"Something's out there."

Theo's grave tone sent apprehension shuddering over her flesh, leaving her skin prickling.

He took her elbow, tugging Willow away from the clearing. "What were you doing out here by yourself? You shouldn't be alone. Next time you want to go out, you let me know."

She bristled, not wanting to confess how unnerved she was now. "I left you a note. Besides, I don't need a babysitter."

"I think you do," he countered. "The bomber doesn't seem to have any reservations about hurting people."

From deep in the woods, a strange popping sound ricocheted off the trees. Birds squawked in protest.

Star barked and lunged on her leash toward the sound.

"She's alerting!" Willow's heart pounded in her throat.

* * *

Pacific Northwest K-9 Unit

Terri Reed's romance and romantic suspense novels have appeared on the *Publishers Weekly* top twenty-five and NPD BookScan top one hundred lists and have been featured in *USA TODAY*, *Christian Fiction* magazine and *RT Book Reviews*. Her books have been finalists for the Romance Writers of America RITA® Award and the National Readers' Choice Award and finalists three times for the American Christian Fiction Writers Carol Award. Contact Terri at terrireed.com or PO Box 19555, Portland, OR 97224.

Books by Terri Reed

Love Inspired Suspense

Buried Mountain Secrets
Secret Mountain Hideout
Christmas Protection Detail
Secret Sabotage
Forced to Flee
Forced to Hide

Rocky Mountain K-9 Unit

Detection Detail

Pacific Northwest K-9 Unit

Explosive Trail

Visit the Author Profile page at LoveInspired.com for more titles.

EXPLOSIVE TRAIL

TERRI REED

LOVE INSPIRED SUSPENSE
INSPIRATIONAL ROMANCE

Special thanks and acknowledgment are given to Terri Reed for her contribution to the Pacific Northwest K-9 Unit miniseries.

LOVE INSPIRED SUSPENSE

INSPIRATIONAL ROMANCE

Recycling programs for this product may not exist in your area.

ISBN-13: 978-1-335-58846-3

Explosive Trail

Copyright © 2023 by Harlequin Enterprises ULC

For questions and comments about the quality of this book, please contact us at CustomerService@Harlequin.com.

Love Inspired
22 Adelaide St. West, 41st Floor
Toronto, Ontario M5H 4E3, Canada
www.LoveInspired.com

Printed in U.S.A.

Charity suffereth long, and is kind; charity envieth not; charity vaunteth not itself, is not puffed up, Doth not behave itself unseemly, seeketh not her own, is not easily provoked, thinketh no evil; Rejoiceth not in iniquity, but rejoiceth in the truth; Beareth all things, believeth all things, hopeth all things, endureth all things.
—*1 Corinthians* 13:4-7

Thank you to the ladies in this series,
Laura Scott, Valerie Hansen, Jodie Bailey, Sharon Dunn,
Jessica R. Patch, Maggie K. Black, Dana Mentink,
Katy Lee and Sharee Stover. Always a joy to work with you.

And a big thank-you to our editor, Emily Rodmell. You're
part guide, part wrangler. We couldn't do it without you.

ONE

June's muted sunlight jabbed through the canopy of towering old-growth conifer trees, lighting the moss-covered trunks and making the verdant green more vibrant on either side of the hiking trail deep in the Hoh Rain Forest of the Olympic National Park of Washington State. A mist hung in the air, dampening Pacific Northwest K-9 officer Willow Bates's hair and beading on the waterproof ballistic vest covering her canine's torso.

Star, a German shorthaired pointer specializing in explosives and weapons detection, sniffed along the narrow trail cut through the thick ferns deep in the woods, searching for explosive devices. Two days ago, such a device had been detonated at the trailhead of a hiking trail near Madison Falls, and a pair of hikers had suffered minor injuries. Thus far no one had claimed responsibility for the bombing.

Anger for the senselessness burned in Willow's gut, digging at an old wound and renewing her determination to protect the park and its inhabitants. A resolve that had already cost her so much.

The ache in her heart throbbed, but she refused to dwell on the past.

Pausing to let Star check out a rotted, felled tree trunk, Willow searched the shadowed forest. A sense of foreboding tightened the muscles across her shoulders. Maybe coming out alone today had been a mistake.

She put her hand on the flak vest covering her abdomen. Not really alone. But still...

Willow's boss, Chief Donovan Fanelli, had sent Willow and another PNK9 officer, Jackson Dean, and his Doberman, Rex, out to patrol the park. Because the Olympic National Park encompassed nearly a million acres of diverse ecosystems ranging from glacier mountains to rain forests to the seventy miles of wild coastline, she and Jackson had taken different sections of the park.

Jackson had with him two of the recruited candidates vying for a spot with the PNK9 unit. The four K-9 officer candidates were trying out by shadowing team members while being evaluated on their skills and to see if they would fit in with the unit. Donovan had told Willow she would have a candidate with her soon, but the remaining two were helping on another case in one of the other national parks in the state that the Pacific Northwest K-9 Unit patrolled.

Normally, Willow enjoyed teaching others about the job that had given her such purpose, but after the news she'd received recently, she was still processing and had set out by herself with Star. Until now, she'd confidently patrolled these beloved trails, determined to keep this part of her world safe. As a kid she'd always imagined this rain forest as being something close to the Shire from Tolkien's books. Becoming a park ranger had been her dream since she was little.

Then somebody had blown up the kiosk at the north park entrance at the exact moment her father had gone to pay for day parking.

Because she'd begged him to take her hiking in the park.

The culprit had never been caught.

The tragedy had formed Willow's future.

Working in the national park gave her a sense of purpose, belonging. And she would not let anything or anyone deter her from protecting this part of her world.

Not even her husband.

Make that her soon-to-be ex-husband.

A stab of grief wrapped up in disappointment hit her smack-dab in the middle of her heart.

Signs of trampled undergrowth redirected her thoughts to the task at hand, and she steered Star over, giving the search command. While Star did her job of sniffing out explosive residue, Willow allowed her senses to grow attuned to her surroundings.

A rustling off to her left had her nerves jumping. Probably one of the many animals that called the rain forest home. Star lost interest in the underbrush and started down the trail. Willow followed, trying hard not to think about the man who'd stolen her heart seven years ago and had broken it more recently.

Star's pace picked up, stretching her leash taut, her nose lifting in the air and then going to the ground. Willow released more of the lead attached to the dog's collar, allowing Star to range farther ahead. The dog was tracking something. Anticipation revved in Willow's veins and refocused her attention.

As a trailhead sign came into view, marking where the trail she was on split into two different trails leading in opposite directions, Willow's stomach knotted.

She lifted up a quick prayer. *Please, Lord, no. Not another one.*

The forensic team had determined the last

explosive device had been set on a timer and attached to the base of the trailhead sign, allowing the suspect to be far from the explosion.

Sure enough, Star stopped at the sign and sat staring at the large wooden block atop a thick post with the names of the trails and arrows pointing away from each other carved into the face. This was Star's passive alert for an explosive device.

A bomb must be attached to the backside of the sign or the post. Willow reined Star close and kept an alert eye out for anyone suspicious; she was thankful there were no hikers in sight. After giving her partner a treat, she hustled away several yards, keeping Star close.

She didn't know what a safe distance would be, since she had no idea the blast radius of whatever device was attached to the sign or how it might trigger. She contemplated peeking to locate the device, to determine size and if it was rigged with a timer or remote detonator, but then decided she would wait for help. Once again, she put her hand over her abdomen. Her baby was safe beneath the flak vest covering Willow's torso.

She needed to be patient. Jackson would send the bomb unit to her location. Until then, she needed to make sure no civilians wandered into the area. She thumbed the mic on her uniform.

The radio crackled, and then Jackson's voice came over the radio. "Willow?"

"Star has alerted. Turning on my GPS locator." She gave him her location and hit the small device attached to her flak vest, knowing it would send a signal back to headquarters and they in turn would send it to Jackson.

"On our way. Calling for reinforcements," Jackson replied, his voice clipped with concern. "Stay safe."

Willow clicked off. Star lifted her head, her tail standing straight up, and her ears twitched. The dog was spooked. A shiver of unease lodged in Willow's chest.

"What is it, girl?" Willow whispered, her gaze sweeping the trail ahead and the shadowed woods, but didn't see what had grabbed Star's attention. Willow didn't have the hearing, the eyesight or the scent receptors of the German shorthaired pointer at her side. Something was out there. An ominous dread skated over Willow's flesh.

Suddenly Star pivoted, staring past Willow at something or someone behind them. Apprehension traipsed up Willow's spine, raising the fine hairs at the nape of her neck.

Star let out a series of vicious barks. Willow's free hand went for her holstered weapon while she hung on tight to the leash tethering her partner to her side. Star lunged past Willow, yanking painfully on Willow's arm. She tightened her hold on the lead and pivoted, but before she could face the threat, she was shoved forward.

She tripped over Star's body and went down hard on the ground, sprawling flat on her belly. The sound of running footsteps crashing through the forest jerked Willow's gaze around. She caught a glimpse of a person in camouflaged, hooded rain gear before they disappeared into the thick undergrowth of tall ferns, young cedars and bushes.

Star ran to the end of her lead, clearly intent on giving chase, but Willow refused to let go of the handle of the long nylon leash.

Just as she righted herself on to all fours, the device Star had alerted on detonated, rocking the ground beneath Willow's hands and knees. Something sharp dug into her shoulder, flattening her on the ground. The concussive sound of the blast assaulted her ears, filling her head, along with Star's sharp whining cry.

Willow lay panting in pain and waiting for help to arrive.

"Where is my wife?" FBI special agent Theo Bates demanded as he charged up to the nurses' station inside the Olympic Medical Center in Port Angeles, Washington.

The sounds of hushed voices and monitors beeping and the distinct anesthetic smell filling his nose, coupled with his fear, made him nauseous. Less than five hours ago, he'd received a call from Donovan Fanelli, the chief of the PNK9 unit, telling him Willow had been injured in a bomb blast in the middle of the Olympic National Park.

Theo had finagled a ride on a private jet from Washington, DC, to Seattle. From there, Chief Donovan Fanelli had transported Theo via helicopter to the helipad atop the hospital. Theo hadn't waited for Donovan to even shut off the helicopter's rotors before he'd jumped out and run full speed into the building.

Now he wanted answers.

"And your wife would be?" The mature nurse stared him down from behind the desk.

"Willow Bates," Theo ground out, desperately trying to rein in his panic and fear. He and his wife might be on the brink of divorce, but he was having a hard time erasing seven years of caring from his heart, despite his unworthiness.

"Give me a moment," the woman said. She typed on a keyboard and then said, "She's in room 303."

Theo turned on the heels of his Florsheim shoes and hurried for the elevator. He jabbed the button. His heart raced, the vibrations working their way through his body. He shook out his hands, trying to get a grip on his emotions. Anxiety twisted his insides like warped metal after a car crash. He'd always known this day might come with Willow working in bomb detection, but the reality of her being hurt was so much worse. He hadn't been here to protect her. In fact, he'd spent the last year pushing her away because he didn't deserve to have the happiness they had once shared.

When the doors of the elevator opened on the third floor, he burst out and marched to the next nurses' station. He flashed his badge, saying, "I'm here to see Willow Bates."

The startled nurse behind the counter pointed down the hall. Theo strode at a fast clip toward his wife's room, the fear of what he might find clamping down on his throat. Images of another person's death, one he was responsible for, taunted his mind, nearly robbing him of breath. The door to room 303 opened, and he collided with a tall, bespectacled doctor.

"Whoa, there," the doctor said, blocking Theo from entering. "Who are you?"

"I'm her husband," Theo told him. *At least for now.*

The doctor's eyes widened, then softened. "She's been given a sedative and is resting."

Theo's heart thumped against his ribs. "What are her injuries?"

"She took a piece of debris in her right shoulder. Thankfully, it missed any vital organs. She's had three stitches. But she and the baby are both fine."

Theo's breath halted in his chest. The need to breathe burned, but he couldn't seem to take in air. *Baby?*

He stumbled backward a few steps as the world spun. He bent and planted his hands on his knees and put his head down as he grappled to make sense of what he'd just heard.

"Let's get you a seat," the doctor said.

Theo held up a hand, waving off the man's concern.

"You can go in and sit with her," the doctor said. "But she will be out of it for a little while."

Theo straightened, his breath returning to some semblance of normal, though his insides were twisting like hands wringing out a wet rag. "How far along is she?"

"Twelve weeks, give or take," the doctor told him. "Congratulations, Daddy."

Roughly around the time they'd separated. The heartbreaking last weekend together, trying to save their marriage, had been three months ago. A knife of pain jabbed Theo in the heart. He was unworthy to be a husband, let alone a father. He didn't deserve any goodness in his life. Was God punishing him?

He barely offered the doctor a nod of acknowledgment before he pushed open the door to Willow's room. He sucked in a sharp breath at the sight of her lying in the bed with her eyes closed, her skin so pale. Her beautiful brown hair splayed over the pillow. An IV was attached to her hand. She lay so still, a real-life Sleeping Beauty. Willow loved fairy tales. He remembered her telling him how her late father used to read to her at night when she was a child.

And now she was pregnant with their child.

His throat closed. He had to work hard to keep the emotions clawing through him from finding purchase. *Hold it together*, he warned himself. Now was not the time to fall apart. He had to stay strong. To stay focused. If he gave the horrors that plagued him any space, he'd splinter into a million pieces. He'd be no good to anyone, let alone the mother of his child.

His child.

The thought sent a new and unfamiliar sort of terror sliding through him.

He walked quietly into the room, unwilling to disturb her, and pulled the chair to her bedside. Taking her free hand, he held tight. Her skin felt cold against his palms. He leaned forward and placed a kiss on her knuckles, giving himself momentary permission to feel something other than pain. Then he bowed his head. The need to pray rose strongly from deep inside. Yet he couldn't form any words or thoughts to lift heavenward.

He didn't deserve God's care.

And now he was adrift, holding on to the only anchor he'd ever wanted or needed. But the chasm between them was wide and deep. A separation of his own making. There was no bridge that would ever close the gap. It was too late for them as a couple. But how would they go forward with a child?

Willow awoke to a sensation of well-being. Strange, considering she'd survived an attack in the woods and stitches in her shoulder where the debris from the bomb had hit her. The meds the paramedics had given her made her brain foggy, and then the doctor had given her more. Her eyelids fluttered open, and the light filtering in through the window made her wince. Her hand ached where the IV had been placed and was hooked up to a bag filled with liquid. A monitor kept track of her heart rate and her pulse.

Her other hand was encased in something warm and soothing.

Turning her head slightly, she let out a silent gasp to find her husband—scratch that—her soon-to-be ex-husband sitting beside her. Theo's head was bowed. A lock of his warm brown hair had fallen over his eyes, keeping her from seeing his expression. He was dressed in his official FBI uniform, not his undercover garb, a navy blue suit with a white shirt and red-white-and-blue-striped tie. On his lapel was the insignia pin that all special agents wore. So handsome. She immediately tamped the attraction down. He was a stranger to her now. Not the man she'd once loved. The man she'd married.

Why was he here? *How* was he here? She glanced around, growing agitated as she realized Star was not in the room. Had she been hurt? Willow searched her memory, but the effort only made her brain hurt. No doubt a side effect from the pain meds and the concussion she'd sustained last month.

She tugged her hand from Theo's grasp.

His head snapped up, his eyes wide then narrowing on her face. "You're awake."

"Thanks, Captain Obvious." An old joke between them. He had a habit of stating what was evident. He'd always told her it helped him to process information.

He gave her that crooked smile she loved. Or rather, had loved at one time. Pain jabbed at her. She turned away from him. "Where's Star?"

At Theo's hesitation, her gaze jerked back to him. Her breath lodged in her throat. *Please God, don't let Star have suffered.*

"I'm sorry," he said. She closed her eyes as grief swamped her. "I didn't think to ask Donovan where they sent Star."

Her gaze met his. "She's not dead?"

He reached for her hand again and squeezed. "No, no. She's fine. I just don't know where she is."

Willow sank back into the cushion of the bed, letting relief wash over her. Belatedly she realized Theo had taken her hand again. But she didn't have the energy to shake him off. Or the willpower.

"When were you going to tell me?"

She stared at the ceiling, counting the little dots in the panels above her. "Tell you what?"

"About the baby?"

TWO

Theo watched Willow closely, even as his heart contracted at the sight of her lying in the hospital bed. He saw the grimace then the resignation in her pretty eyes as she slowly met his gaze.

"Who told you?"

Her soft voice wrapped around him, so familiar, yet there was a huge distance between them. A gap of his own making. Guilt spasmed in his chest. "The doctor."

She turned away from him and stared toward the window. Her profile so beloved and well-known. The straight line of her nose, the curve of her cheekbone.

He reached forward and with the tip of his finger under her chin drew her gaze back to him. Though he didn't blame her for keeping the information from him, he still pressed. "Willow?"

Her eyes filled with unshed tears, but there was a strength in her gaze that spoke of the officer and woman who unflinching met danger head-on. Usually.

"Eventually."

The word slammed into him. Removing his finger from her chin and his hand from hers, he rose and began to pace, reliving the last time they'd seen each other.

He had been on a seven-month undercover assignment in the South trying to plug an opioid pipeline on the Eastern Seaboard that hadn't allowed time for anything personal beyond a few text messages. It had been grueling, and he'd been nearly manic in his pursuit of shutting down the drugs and avenging the death of his informant.

Then his boss had pulled him off the case and ordered him home, against Theo's protests. That was three months ago.

He shouldn't have returned to Port Angeles—and to Willow—because he couldn't hide his frustration and anger. Or the debilitating guilt and shame eating away at him.

After the last weekend together, she'd told him to leave and given him back her wedding rings. Her hurt and bewilderment palpable after numerous attempts to pry him open like an oyster plucked from the sea. Only he didn't have a pearl inside. Only darkness. He didn't blame her for sending him away. He was unfit to be a husband. Barely fit to be an agent.

She had filed for divorce the next week.

He'd howled with anguish and resisted the urge—no, need—to run back to her, to ask her to reconsider. He didn't deserve reconsideration. Instead, he'd tucked her wedding band and diamond ring away for good.

"We don't have to think about the future right now," he told her. He needed time to process this revelation of her pregnancy and all that bringing a child into the world would mean for both of them. "You need to heal. Then we will talk about what comes next."

"You've made it clear there is no future for you and me by shutting me out. You left our marriage long before I asked you to leave," she said, her gaze hard, her voice flat. "Moving on is the best thing for both of us."

An arrow of heartbreak embedded itself deep inside, the pain radiating outward forcing him to say, "But a child changes everything."

"Does it?" She cocked her head to the side, her gaze searching his face.

He purposely shuddered his expression, not wanting her to glimpse creeping darkness within.

"Are you willing to stop doing undercover

work?" Her tone challenged and poked at him. "Are you willing to open up and let me back in?"

He ground his back teeth. He couldn't. He had a debt to pay. Even then, he didn't know if he'd ever be the man he once was. The man she'd once loved. They were strangers now, tied together by a child.

Her gaze dropped, her expression softening to sadness. "I can't do this anymore. I'm tired."

There was a knock on the door before it opened. Chief Donovan Fanelli walked in, dressed in the green uniform of the PNK9 unit, with his Malinois by his side. Theo had great respect for the tall, lanky man who'd founded the unit. Several other members of the team filed in behind their boss. Theo recognized Officer Jackson Dean, a muscular, towering man with blue eyes, and his Doberman, a sleek and muscled beast named Rex. Theo didn't know the other two officers, a tall blond man with green eyes and a fit-looking woman with a pixie haircut who vaguely remind him of the unit's technical expert. Each had a canine at their side and hung back near the door.

After the pleasantries of shaking hands with the chief and Jackson, Jackson introduced the two candidates vying for a spot with the unit, Owen Hannington and Veronica Eastwood.

Theo was right—Veronica had to be related to Jasmin Eastwood, the team's tech expert.

"This is Willow's husband," Jackson said. "FBI special agent Theo Bates."

It was like a knife to the chest to hear himself referred to still as Willow's husband. Soon he wouldn't have that claim. Needing a moment, Theo excused himself and went out into the hall. He took in several deep breaths before calling his boss to explain the situation.

"Sounds like they could use your help," his boss said.

Theo hadn't considered the possibility. It would allow him to be close to Willow if he stayed and helped find this bomber. But the cost would be high. He and Willow would be forced together. She carried his child. He owed it to her and his baby to put aside his own torment to protect them. Resolved not to leave Willow's side until she was completely out of harm's way, he said, "I could be useful here."

"Good. Saves me from having to put you on formal leave," his boss said.

Theo winced. He knew he'd been called back to Quantico after this last three-month stint undercover to be reprimanded. He'd bent a few rules in his quest to find the source of the opioids, but it had gained them valuable information that had led another team to a distribution warehouse in Florida.

"Until something more pressing arises, stay in Washington State. Catch this bomber and get your head on straight."

"Yes, sir." Willow wouldn't be happy to learn he was staying and that he was going to be her shadow for the duration. He didn't doubt her abilities as an officer. They'd met while working a case together. They both had jobs that required them to act and to be in the line of fire. Though he'd worried for her, he'd never been fearful. Until now.

He told himself it was only because of the child. Not because the thought of losing her forever filled him with dread.

"Where is Star? Is she okay?" Willow stared at her boss, Chief Donovan Fanelli, meeting his brown eyes as worry chomped through her.

"She's fine," Jackson assured her. A former US marshal, he had intense blue eyes that seemed to see everything. "No injuries from the blast. She's at the training center right now with Peyton."

Willow relaxed in relief. Peyton Burns, the lead trainer for the unit, was good people. She would take care of Star.

"Can you tell us what happened?" Donovan asked.

"We were on the Hoh River Trail, where it junctions with High Divide Trail, when Star alerted," she told them. "That's when I called Jackson. Then Star reacted with aggression at someone behind me. Before I could react, I was shoved forward. I guess I tripped over Star. Then the device detonated. After that it's a bit fuzzy because of the pain meds. I remember being loaded into the ambulance, but that's about it."

"Did you get a look at the person who pushed you?" Donovan asked.

"No. I caught a glimpse, but it was more of a shadow, and I heard the person run away into the forest. Star wanted to give chase, but I held on to her."

"Good thinking," Donovan said. "You protected your partner. Star is not cross-trained in apprehension. You did good."

His approval and praise filled her with pleasure. "The suspect still got too close."

"The device seems to be similar to the one that detonated a few days ago," Jackson stated.

Donovan's jaw set in a grim line. "We have a serial bomber on our hands, people."

Anxiety twisted in Willow's chest. She couldn't let the past repeat itself. She couldn't lose someone else she loved or let more innocent people be hurt. She had to catch this guy.

The door to the room opened, and Theo walked back in. Willow couldn't take her eyes off him. But it had always been that way from the moment they'd met. He'd been working a case out of Seattle and needed help from the unit. Their romance had been a whirlwind, and she'd thought she'd finally found someone who would love her, want her and need her without conditions.

Her few other romantic relationships before Theo had come with expectations she'd not been able to meet—mostly, giving up her career path. Not Theo.

Their commitment to protecting their world had been a cemented bond. One that had eventually crushed them.

The first few years their marriage had been wonderful. He'd moved to Port Angeles, where they'd bought a house. They both loved their careers and each other. She couldn't have asked for more.

She didn't know what had happened a year ago, but he'd changed. Become withdrawn and moody, and he'd lashed out at the tiniest irritation.

The time between seeing each other grew farther and farther apart, just as the gap in their relationship had widened until she couldn't take it any longer. Being around him hurt. She'd begged him to tell her what she'd done, but he'd only grow more agitated and escape to another undercover assignment.

Despite how much she'd prayed and tried to be understanding, she finally had to protect herself by ending the marriage. Hardening her heart was painful, but it grew easier as time went on.

She jerked her gaze away from Theo, meeting Veronica's. The other woman gave her an encouraging smile. Willow wished she could return the favor, especially after the weird incident last month with Veronica's weapon and badge disappearing. Thankfully, she'd found both, but not in the place she'd left them. But at the moment, it was all Willow could do to keep her eyes open.

Though the sedative had worn off, the pain in her shoulder where the piece of wood had cut through her skin caused her grief. Not to mention the ache in her heart at having Theo here. She didn't want to feel anything for him. She needed him to leave. There was no reason for him to be here. She was fine. Without him.

"A serial bomber is exactly why I'm staying," Theo announced to the room, clearly having heard Donovan's statement.

Willow stared at him as shock stole her breath. Their gazes locked. "Excuse me?"

Without breaking eye contact, Theo said to Donovan, "Chief, you'll be getting a call from my boss, requesting I stay to help catch the bomber."

Donovan's gaze bounced between Theo and Willow and back to Theo. "All hands on deck. I like it. You and Willow can work together."

"Wait! What?" Willow couldn't believe her boss would give that directive. But of course, Donovan didn't know that her marriage to Theo was ending. She'd only confided in her friend Mara Gilmore, the unit's rookie criminal evidence technician.

Her friend who was accused of a double homicide—the murders of her ex-boyfriend and his new girlfriend.

A fresh wave of anguish washed over Willow.

She didn't believe Mara had committed the crimes and wished there was some way for her to help the woman. But Mara had been seen running away from the crime scene by two PNK9 officers and was still out there, hiding from the authorities.

Unfortunately, things were stacking up against Mara. Her bracelet with a gold *M* had been found at the crime scene. And despite Star having located a department-issued weapon, sans fingerprints, buried near the murdered victims, which was a ballistics match, Willow knew the evidence was circumstantial at best. If only Mara would contact her.

"Is there a problem?" Donovan asked, his gaze boring into Willow.

Only her fellow PNK9 unit member Colt Maxwell and his new fiancée, Brooke Stevens, a park ranger in Mount Rainier National Park, were aware of Willow's condition. They'd worked closely on a case last month, and Willow had opened up to Brooke and Colt.

Well, now Theo knew, too.

Willow silently willed Theo to keep the information of her pregnancy to himself. If her boss knew, he might take her off the job. The doctor had told her she and the baby were fine and there was no issue with her continuing to work as long as she stayed away from bomb blasts. *Ha!*

But she wasn't out of her first trimester yet. There was still a possibility that she might… She shied away from that thought. Best not to borrow trouble.

At her continued silence, Donovan's expression turned stern. "This bomber doesn't seem in the least bit worried about who he hurts. And if the bomber is the one who pushed you, then he or she knows who you are. We don't know if the bomber will come after you. Having an FBI special agent around will be an asset. Plus, I'm going to assign you two of the candidates to be with you at all times. They're fully trained general K-9 officers," he added with a nod at the contenders.

Willow swallowed the lump of agitation forming in her throat. At least there would be a buffer—she wouldn't be alone with Theo. His presence stirred too many unwelcome emotions, making her long for something she couldn't have—a life with him and their child.

The sooner they caught this bomber, the better. Then Theo would go back to his life working undercover, which seemed to be more important to him than his wife. And Willow could go back to hers, raising their child alone and spending the rest of her life doing her best not to miss the version of Theo she'd once loved.

Several hours later, Theo bundled Willow, now wearing hospital scrubs and a jacket from Veronica, into a borrowed PNK9 vehicle. Since the moment her boss had basically ordered her to work with him, she had been unnaturally silent. Donovan and other team members clearly noticed and kept giving him strange looks full of questions. Obviously, she hadn't told her unit that they were on the brink of divorce or that she'd recently found out she was pregnant.

He figured it was her tale to tell at this point.

Honestly, he hadn't mentioned their impending divorce to anyone, either. It was too personal and would lead to places Theo had no intention of going. He stuffed the bad down, because if he let it out, he didn't believe he'd survive.

As he navigated the SUV out of the hospital parking lot, he shook off the memories threatening to drag him under and said, "Are you comfortable? Do you need anything before we hit the highway?"

She held up the bottle of water the nurse had given her before leaving the hospital. "I'm fine." Then she sat back and closed her eyes.

Apparently, she didn't want any more conversation with him than necessary. But they did need to talk. He needed to process the fact that he was going to be a father.

Driving in silence, provided too much thinking time and only served to make his nerves jumpy. Glancing at Willow, he hesitated to bring up their impending parenthood. Maybe getting her to talk about the case would ease her into opening up to him about their child and would fill the quiet void where his mind tended to relive the horrors that haunted him.

"I know you've already gone through this with Chief Fanelli but tell me more about the bomb today. It might help me understand the nature of the bomber."

She let out a heavy sigh, then straightened in her seat, all business. "This was the second bomb in three days. The first was on a trail, where two hikers were injured. Both times the device was attached to a trailhead marker. What could that mean?"

"Maybe the bomber is trying to confuse hikers. Wanting them to get lost in the wilderness."

Willow finally looked at him. "To what end?"

He shrugged. "It's only a theory at this point. When we get to the training center, I'll call Bartholomew and ask him to send over his report on the devices." The unit's head forensic tech, Bartholomew Davis, was a friend and top-notch at his job. "His conclusions might give us some more information about who this person is. Often bombers leave some sort of signature behind."

Wincing at having told her something she already knew, he was thankful she didn't tease him again about his propensity to state the obvious.

"I think Star and I might've startled him after he placed the second bomb. Why else would he have pushed me before running away?"

"As your boss said, we don't know if the person who pushed you is the person who planted the bomb."

Willow shifted in her seat to face him fully, clearly engaged now. She loved the work, which had been one of the many things about her that had drawn him to her in the first place. "But they have to be, don't you think? Two people out there for nefarious purposes? Doubtful. Unless they're working together."

"Without knowing how long that device had been attached to the trailhead, we won't have a complete picture. It would be helpful if Bartholomew can narrow down a time frame of when the bomb was planted."

"If anyone can, it's Bart."

"I'm glad you weren't hurt worse. I understand from Jackson that you turned on your homing beacon." The device had been one of their concessions early on in their marriage. He'd been naturally concerned for her and Star going out on patrol without it. Too many things could happen. Step wrong and twist an ankle. Or an encounter with a bear or other wild animal. The GPS tracker was quick and effective.

"It finally came in handy," she murmured.

He could feel her steady gaze on him, and it took all his willpower not to turn toward her. Instead, he concentrated on following the navigation directions. Soon they were at the training center. Willow had once told him that a very rich philanthropist, Roland Evans, had funded a federal grant to start the PNK9 Unit, comprised of federal officers to safeguard the state's national parks. The grant included money for a training center in the city of Olympia behind the unit's headquarters.

Theo had read about Chief Donovan Fanelli and his canine, Sarge, when Donovan had been a National Park Service K-9 officer and had caught the man who'd killed the wife of the philanthropist, Roland Evans.

Theo parked in front of the training center and turned off the engine. Willow popped open the door, but he placed a hand on her forearm. "I'll come around."

She made a face. "I'm capable of getting out of the car on my own."

"Humor me, please."

Her gaze dropped to his hand and then rose back to his face. The longing in her eyes nearly undid him. He fought the urge to pull her close, like he had a million times before. But that was then, when he had a claim on her. He didn't now. He didn't deserve her. He released his hold on her and jogged around to her side of the vehicle and helped her out of the passenger seat, noting the tight lines around her mouth as she maneuvered to a standing position.

She was so tough and strong, and she wanted the world to believe that nothing could ever get to her. But he knew the truth. She had a vulnerable core she let few see. He'd once been counted among the few. Losing the special place in her life left him with an ache so deep he doubted it would ever heal. But it was better to keep her at a distance than to drag her into his dark world.

Shaking off his hand, she strode for the training center doors. He had no choice but to follow in her wake. When she reached the entrance, he hustled forward in time to push the door open, allowing her to pass through with a softly spoken "Thank you."

"Willow!" A pretty, petite redhead, wearing the green uniform of the unit, greeted her. Over her shirt she had on a vest that bulged with toys and no doubt treats.

Theo recognized Peyton Burns, the lead trainer for the whole canine unit. She rushed to hug Willow, who shifted so that she could give the other woman a one-armed hug on her uninjured side.

Peyton drew back. "You're hurt?"

"A few stitches. Nothing to worry about."

Theo didn't like the way Willow downplayed her injury. She and the baby could have been more seriously hurt, or worse, if she had been closer to the bomb. The very idea had a wave of terror crashing over him and cresting in his lungs, making breathing difficult. What if she'd died? Another person he'd sworn to protect harmed because he hadn't kept his promise.

"Hi, Theo. Seeing you is a pleasant surprise," Peyton said.

Snapping out of the dark hole threatening to engulf him, he managed to reply, "Good to see you, too, Peyton."

"Where's Star?" Willow's impatience rang in her tone.

Peyton raised her eyebrows but gestured toward the training ring. "Go on in. We're socializing the puppies and introducing them to the terrain in and around Olympic National Park."

Willow's beautiful face lit up, and she clapped her hands with glee, then hurried into the training center arena. Theo hung back, letting Star and Willow have their reunion while he watched through the glass door. The German shorthaired pointer stood in the center of three adorable bloodhound puppies who'd been gifted to the unit as future police dogs.

Star had been nosing the long, floppy ear of a puppy when her head came up. Obviously, she'd caught Willow's scent. The dog pivoted and let out a high-pitched bark, then ran full speed toward Willow.

Concerned that Star would hurt Willow, Theo opened the training ring door and stepped inside but paused as Willow quickly stopped and put up a hand. "Halt."

Star skidded to a stop at Willow's feet. Willow made another gesture and said, "Down."

Star dropped to her belly on the ground. Willow sat on the ground and patted her legs, inviting Star to come forward. She wrapped her arms around Star's neck, smiling as Star licked her face. Then Star's super sniffer lifted, and she moved to Willow's side, her blue eyes zeroing in on Theo.

Letting out a happy bark, which warmed Theo's heart, Star rushed forward, but before she could reach Theo, Willow whistled and the dog paused with her snout forward and her tail straight back. Willow whistled again, and the dog slowed to a trot until she reached Theo.

Theo went down on one knee and petted Star. The dog relaxed, leaning against him. The amount of comfort oozing off the dog and settling around him helped to calm Theo's inner turmoil. Theo bowed his head to touch Star's forehead, absorbing as much peace as he could from the dog.

When Theo lifted his head, his gaze snagged on Willow's arrested expression. He swallowed back the surge of yearning, forcing himself to look away.

"She's missed you."

Willow's soft voice wrapped around Theo. It was on the tip of his tongue to ask if her handler had missed him, too. But that wouldn't be fair. He'd ruined his marriage. There was no going back. They had to heal so they could formulate a plan for their child's future.

Willow turned away and headed for the bloodhound puppies, who were tumbling over one another at the other end of the arena. Two of the puppies ambled forward, plopping down on their tummies and rolling over for belly rubs when she reached them. Theo was content to watch Willow, memorizing the curve of her cheek, the graceful way she moved. Her beauty created an ache in his chest.

A smile spread across Willow's face, and Theo's heart jammed in his throat.

How long had it been since he'd seen that much joy and happiness on her face? A long time. Because of him. He'd done that to her.

Crushed her love for him. But he couldn't help it. It was better for her. For him.

But now a child was involved. And he had no idea what to do. How could he be a father when he'd failed at being a husband? Failed at his job?

Giving Star a last good scrub behind her ears, Theo said, "Let's go meet these puppies."

Peyton joined him and they walked to where the puppies now gathered around Willow, who was sitting in the dirt again, despite how sore she must be from being caught in the blast. The puppies climbed all over her. Star moved to sit beside Willow, a silent sentry watching the little ones but making no move to curb their pleasure.

Willow looked up at Peyton. "They are so much cuter in person than in the photos the chief showed us."

"That one's named Chief." Peyton pointed to one pup that was trying to bite his own tail. "And this one—" Peyton scooped up a wiggling dog. "Is Ranger. You're holding Agent."

"Where did they come from?" Theo asked, thinking how much money the dogs were worth.

"Roland Evans gifted them, and his grandson named them." Peyton set Ranger down. The dog tripped over his long, floppy ear and rolled away. "They will be scent trained to work the parks. Oh, I almost forgot," Peyton said, digging into the pocket of her jacket and producing a cell phone. "This was tucked into Star's vest when she arrived."

"It must've fallen out of my pocket during the blast." Willow took the phone, checking the call log, then listening to a message. She gave a small gasp.

Theo went down on one knee beside her. "What is it?"

Willow's stunned gaze lifted to his. "I missed a call from Mara Gilmore."

Why was the woman who was accused of a double homicide calling Willow?

THREE

Leaving the training center with Star in the back compartment of the borrowed SUV and Theo driving, Willow tried to contain her upset at having missed the call from Mara. Why had Mara reached out? Where was she? Hurt? Safe? Frightened?

Willow called the phone number back, lifting a prayer Mara would answer.

"Hello?" a female voice, not Mara's, answered.

Pushing back her disappointment and introducing herself, Willow said, "Who is this I'm speaking to?"

"Ester Williams. What can I do for you, Officer?"

"I'm looking for Mara Gilmore. She called me from this number."

"Oh, is that her name?" Ester said. "I was shopping at our local grocery store, Smithy's, when she begged to borrow my cell phone."

Willow's stomach clenched with concern. "Where are you located?"

"Packwood, Washington."

A small town an hour outside of Mount Rainier. How had Mara found her way there?

Thanking the woman, Willow immediately reached out to the PNK9 unit's tech expert, Jasmin Eastwood.

"Willow? Are you okay? I heard what happened." Jasmin said, no doubt having seen Willow's name appear on her caller ID.

"I'm good. Jasmin, Mara tried to call me." Willow explained about missing the call and from where it originated. "Can you check CCTV in the store and the area? We must find her and help her."

There was a moment's hesitation, then Jasmin said, "I have to turn this information over to the National Parks Crime Scene Unit."

Willow was frustrated that because Mara was a part of their team and the perceived conflict of interest, PNK9's forensic team couldn't work on the case. "Do what you must. Do we know which of our officers might be close to go interview Ester Williams?"

"I'll talk to Donovan," Jasmin promised.

"Thank you." Nervousness fluttered in Willow's stomach as she hung up. Not only was she worried for her friend, but also by the idea of Theo coming home to the house they'd once shared. She'd made several changes in the house, trying to make it less painful to have Theo gone.

Changing the artwork on the walls and re-arranging the kitchen cupboards hadn't been enough. She could never erase the ache of longing for her husband. But she'd learned over the past year to deal with the loneliness. He'd made the choice to leave her, to go under-cover for long stretches of time. For the past year their relationship had disintegrated until she wasn't sure why they'd ever married. She couldn't even articulate what went wrong.

After an undercover assignment, it seemed a switch had flipped in Theo. He'd become dis-tant and irritable and stopped talking to her. He'd shut her out, making her feel unloved and unwanted. He kept volunteering for undercover assignments. They hadn't seen much of each other, and when he did come home, they only seemed to argue.

The last week they spent together, three months ago, ended in more hurt and anger. Exhausted from the turmoil, she decided she couldn't live like this anymore and it was time to end their marriage. She'd had to harden her heart, crushing the love she'd once held for Theo in order to file for divorce.

Deep inside, she feared she was letting God down, but her mental health was suffering under the weight of her decaying marriage.

Stewing over the drive back to Port Angeles had her nerves stretched taut.

Now, watching Theo maneuver through late-afternoon traffic with the familiarity that came from having lived in the seaside town, she focused on her friend Mara rather than the awkwardness that was sure to come once they reached their destination.

Mara Gilmore was a fairly new crime scene tech with the unit. Willow had liked the younger woman, and they had hit it off right away. They'd become friends and confidantes. Mara was the only one Willow had talked to about her marriage not being the ideal everybody assumed it was. The Mara Willow had come to know was sweet and kind and analytical. There was no way she would have committed the double homicide—of her ex and his new girlfriend in Mount Rainier National Park. There had to be some kind of mistake.

Willow slanted a glance at her husband. Her chest knotted. Soon-to-be ex-husband. Why couldn't she get the idea of not being married to Theo through her thick skull?

Because it hurt too much to think about the years they'd both invested in each other and how it all came crumbling down so easily. A marriage built on quicksand.

But he was here now. And he had the expertise to help her aid Mara.

"I know you never met Mara," Willow started. "But I know her fairly well. I believe in my heart she didn't kill anyone. Mara's reserved and keeps to herself, to the point some people falsely assume she's snooty, but she's not."

For a moment, Theo remained silent. Willow waited, knowing he was processing and considering his words, as was his way.

"If she didn't commit these crimes, then why did she flee from the crime scene and not turn herself in?"

A question that undoubtedly had been running through the minds of every member of the K-9 unit. Willow didn't have the answer. She gritted her teeth with frustration.

"If she didn't do it, as you believe," Theo said softly, "what other explanation could there be?"

"She's being framed." Willow voiced the thought she hadn't dared say until now. But due to his experience with the FBI, Theo was the only one who might believe her. Might help her prove Mara innocent. With him, her ideas and thoughts were safe. At least her work-related ones. Which only made losing him that much more excruciating.

"Then the question becomes, by whom?"

Gratified he didn't dismiss her claim outright, she said, "There's a suspect pool. Many of the competitive lodge owners around the parks could barely conceal their anger at Stacey Stark. Apparently, she'd tried to steal guests from them in the past."

"Alibis?"

Willow hated to admit it, but she said, "They all have alibis. But those could be faked, right?"

"Could be. Worth looking into with a fresh perspective. Though whoever committed this crime has to be somebody who is close to Stacey and the other victim," Theo stated. "Tell me what you know about these two people."

Acid burned in Willow's stomach. "Jonas Digby and Stacey Stark had recently started dating. From what we understand, Stacey had recently become a Christian."

"Was there anyone who didn't like that they were dating?"

Willow rubbed at the spot beneath her breastbone where the burn of anxiety threatened to eat her alive. All the stress probably wasn't good for the baby, but she had to be honest with Theo. "Mara and Jonas had dated."

Theo pulled into the driveway of the small two-bedroom cottage they had once shared in a residential neighborhood one block from the ocean. He cut the engine and turned to face her. The intensity in his brown eyes had her worry ratcheting up. "Did their relationship end badly?"

Grimacing, she nodded. "I overheard Mara tell him he couldn't treat people so poorly and not expect consequences. But when I asked her about it, she said Jonas broke up with her, though Mara knew they were headed that way… She had suspicions he was seeing someone else. Stacey, as it turns out."

"That sounds like a good motive."

"No." Willow had to make him understand. "Mara's anger over the breakup was about his dishonesty, rather than the actual ending of their relationship."

"She may have told you that, but in her heart…" Theo shook his head. "You can never know what's in someone else's heart."

Not wanting to acknowledge the truth in his words, or how they applied to the two of them as well as Mara, Willow said, "There are enough people who know about Mara's close ties to the couple. They also know her comings and goings enough to frame her."

Theo went silent again, his gaze tender, making Willow's heart pound.

"Would you like me to look at the case files?"

Her heart melted at his offer. She didn't want to need Theo, but he had the expertise, and he was here, so why not utilize him? The team had been investigating around the clock, and Willow wished she could devote more time to trying to help exonerate her friend. She and Theo could work on both the serial bomber case and Mara's case. "Yes. Maybe you could find a crack in the alibis. Or uncover someone we've overlooked."

Willow knew that Mara's half brother, Asher Gilmore, an officer with the K-9 unit, was also looking for a way to clear Mara's name. But the two hadn't grown up together and weren't close, and Willow got the feeling that Asher didn't know what to think about the murders. Sometimes Willow felt like the only one who truly believed Mara was innocent.

Theo put his hand over hers, his touch both warm and comforting. "For you, I would do anything."

Her breath stalled in her chest. How did she respond to that? She pushed back the welling of affection flooding her system. It was too painful to allow it any room. Where had his concern and caring been over the past year? Why had he pushed her away and shut her out of his life?

Releasing her abruptly, he popped open his door and jumped out. She stayed rooted to the seat, giving herself a moment to collect her composure. Then he opened her door and offered her his hand. Steeling herself against the barrage of emotions she knew would come with the contact, she slipped her hand into his.

Their palms met like a kiss, sending waves of sensation up her arm. A deep yearning for the way their marriage had once been threatened to overwhelm her, but she couldn't let it. The past needed to stay firmly in the past. He'd crushed her heart once. She wasn't about to let him do it again. Eventually, she'd find a way to function without the constant ache of loss.

She quickly climbed out of the vehicle and tugged her hand free. She released Star from the back compartment. The dog ran around the front yard, apparently happy to be home.

As they approached the house, Willow's agitation grew. How would Theo take the changes she'd made? Would he like the color she'd used inside or the new furniture she'd purchased?

She shoved the questions away. Why did it matter what Theo thought? She couldn't let her emotions control her life. To be fair, last month the doctor had told her to expect a roller-coaster ride of emotions.

After taking a blow to the head from an unhinged woman during a case and ending up in the hospital, Willow had confessed to the doctor she hadn't been feeling well for several weeks. The doctor had insisted on running some tests. And the results had shocked Willow to the core. She was pregnant. That last, heartbreakingly poignant visit with Theo had resulted in an unexpected joy.

Willow had called Theo immediately after being discharged from the hospital, despite the late hour. But she'd been unable to reach him. He'd been on another undercover assignment, according to his boss when she'd called him next.

Theo had never called back.

Pain, so sharp her breath caught, cut deep, making her steps falter. Theo captured her elbow. The gesture at once familiar, tender and unexpected. She fought the urge to lean against him for support. He was no longer hers, and she didn't need him.

Resigning herself to being uncomfortable with Theo as a guest in their home, she unlocked the door. As she walked inside, she placed a hand over her abdomen. The material of the nurses' scrubs she'd been given at the hospital itched her skin.

Tears burned the backs of her eyes. She wanted to do right by her child. Their child. She just had no clue how, or what the future would look like. She'd spent countless hours praying for guidance, but God's silence made her fear He had turned His back on her.

Stepping into the house he'd once called home, Theo's heart lurched. Everything seemed different. Gone was the old leather sofa and recliner that had once taken up most of the living room. Instead, there were two small love seats in a light silver color. One, he noted, had the electric controls on the side for a recliner. Even Star had a new plush bed and a slew of new toys. The walls had been painted a light gray, covering up the sweet mocha-almond color they had labored together to paint when they had first bought the house.

Had she done the new painting on her own? Or had she had help? Was there a new man in her life?

A particular kind of burn spread through his chest. One he identified as jealousy. But he'd relinquished his claim on her when he'd left the last time. His words still echoed in his mind so hurtful, so wrong. *I don't want to be here.*

"You can put your stuff in the spare room," she said in a brittle tone as she walked down the hall toward their bedroom.

No, not their bedroom. Her room now. He didn't belong here anymore. Seeing the changes, witnessing how she'd already moved on, proved the fact.

Even knowing she was beyond ready to put their marriage behind them, he couldn't stop his need to help and protect her. He hated seeing her so upset. Witnessing how deeply her compassion and dedication to those she cared about ran were one of the many things that made her so attractive. She'd shown devotion and loyalty to her teammates. To the case they had worked on all those many years ago when they'd first met.

And then she had shown that same sort of compassion and dedication to him.

She could have derailed his career when he'd first been asked to go undercover, but she'd been encouraging. His biggest cheerleader. She understood his ambition to be more, to be better and to prove to his father that he could make a difference by joining the FBI.

And what had his ambition earned him?

Heartache. Torment. Proof that he should have stayed in his lane, doing his job here in Washington State rather than accepting the assignment to help stop the illicit opioids fueling a devastating epidemic plaguing the country.

If he'd not taken that first assignment, Xavier Jones would still be alive.

Theo and Willow would still be happily married.

Theo wouldn't be tormented by nightmares.

He walked down the hall, opening the door to the room that had once been an office they had shared. Now it was an exercise room. Blue rubber mats covered the floor, and a TV had been mounted on the wall. There was a fancy bicycle affixed to a trainer stand for indoor cycling in the corner. Dumbbells and exercise bands and a big exercise ball lined up against the wall beneath the window.

But what had him catching his breath and made his heart sink into his stomach was the stack of boxes with his name printed on them in Willow's handwriting.

He backed out of the room. He couldn't do this. Staying here would be too awkward. Painful even.

Willow changed into fresh clothes but hesitated in returning to the living room, where Theo waited. She didn't know how to do this. To be so close to him, yet they were strangers.

She picked up the phone and dialed her mother.

"Hello, sweetheart. How are you?" Melanie Branson's voice soothed Willow.

Sitting on the bed, Willow said, "I've been better." She relayed the events and that now she was at home, safe and sound with Theo.

"I'm so glad you weren't hurt worse. Should I come over?"

Affection filled Willow. "No. Theo and I need to work this out."

"Have you told him about the baby?"

"He knows." She could only imagine the shock he'd experienced to learn from the doctor that she was pregnant.

"I'm going to say this again—I strongly urge you to seek counseling. You and Theo. You're going to be parents, whether you stay married or not."

Willow sighed. "I'll talk to him about going to therapy." Though how she'd broach the subject she didn't know. He was a proud man. She didn't believe he'd go willingly.

"Even if he won't, you should," her mom pressed, as she had for the past three months. "But I know you two will do what's best."

"Thanks, Mom. I love you. I've got to go."

After hanging up, Willow contemplated her next move. She didn't know what to do about

Theo. She sent up a prayer that God would direct them. Her priority for the moment had to be stopping the bomber from striking again.

Theo paced the living room. His mind whirled with possible solutions to the situation with his soon-to-be ex-wife. Staying here would be torturous. He stopped abruptly when Willow finally reappeared, having changed into jeans that hugged her curves and a lightweight sweater in a soft yellow that complemented her skin tone and the highlights in her hair. Achingly beautiful. No longer his.

He blurted out, "It would be best if we moved to the Stark Lodge at the main entrance of Olympic National Park. We could work from there. It would allow us to be closer to the park." And give them space.

Her eyes widened, and her mouth opened. He expected a protest, but instead, she said, "Brilliant idea. That's why you get paid the big bucks."

He wasn't sure how to respond. Was she as uncomfortable as he was? Was she struggling to hold back the memories of what they'd once shared the same way he was struggling? Or did she want to keep him out of her life?

"I'll pack a bag." She gave him a look that he

couldn't interpret. "Can you pack Star's food and essentials?"

"Are they—"

"In the same place? Yes."

He supposed that was as much of an acknowledgment as he was going to get that she had made so many changes to her life. Did he dare ask if she was seeing someone else?

Deciding it was none of his business, that he'd given up the right to know about her life when he agreed to a divorce, he gave her a nod and set about packing up Star's equipment and food. He packed enough for a week, though he didn't anticipate they would be at the Stark Lodge that long. At least he hoped not. Being close to Willow was wreaking havoc on his emotions and his heart.

Soon, they were back on the road, headed to the Stark Lodge, leaving Port Angeles behind as the terrain turned woodsier. They followed the coast road and then cut inland toward the main entrance. He pulled into the parking lot of the Stark Lodge.

The lodge itself was a beautiful structure that stood three stories tall with a covered front porch, all polished wood and a steeply pitched roof. It reminded Theo of a huge log mansion plopped down in the middle of the forest.

"Let's secure rooms and then we can un-pack," he said as he hopped out of the vehicle.

This time Willow did not wait for him to help her out of the passenger seat. She climbed out on her own and went to the back compartment to release Star. Theo grabbed their bags and Star's bed. After leashing Star up and letting her take a moment on the patch of grass near the front entrance, they headed inside.

The lodge lobby was beautifully appointed, with a huge stone fireplace at one end with several comfortable couches and chairs facing it, inviting guests to relax before a roaring fire. Hardwood floors were covered in brightly colored area rugs and led to the reception desk and the bank of elevators. A small restaurant off to one side had a specials board out front of the hostess podium. The whole effect was a rustic-meets-luxe vibe. Theo liked the place.

At the front desk, Theo requested two rooms next to one another. He wanted Star and Willow close enough for him to protect them, yet afford him a little bit of distance.

"I'm sorry, the only close-together rooms we have left available are in our presidential suite," the young woman said. Her name tag read Janet. "It has two bedrooms on opposite ends of a living room and kitchenette."

Theo looked to Willow, assessing how she

felt about sharing the space. "I'm okay with it if you are."

Willow bit her lip then nodded. "Sounds great."

They secured the suite. Janet gave them each a key. As they headed away from the counter toward the elevator, Star veered off to their left, her nose shuffling along the edge of a closed door that read Stairwell. Then Star pawed at the floor, her nails making a rat-a-tat sound against the hardwood.

Theo's heart thumped in his chest. "Could there be explosives in the stairwell?"

Willow shook her head and reeled Star close to her side. "That's not her explosive alert. That's her weapons alert."

Theo put his hand on his holstered Glock beneath his coat jacket. What would he find behind the stairwell door?

FOUR

That's her weapons alert.

Willow's breathing accelerated as she held Star close. Her words hung in the air. Was the inn storing weapons? Had Stacey Stark, who had co-owned the three Stark lodges with a business partner, been involved in something shady that resulted in her death? How did Mara fit into this?

Theo tested the stairwell doorknob. Locked.

"The front desk," Willow said, already turning toward the reception area.

Theo fell into step beside her. When they reached the front desk, the wide-eyed clerk behind the counter stared at them with surprise. "Is everything okay?"

"Janet, I need you to unlock the door to that stairwell," Theo said.

"Oh. I don't have keys to that stairwell," Janet said, her voice trembling slightly. "It's private."

"Who does have keys?" Impatience laced Theo's words.

A shadow crossed Janet's face. "The hotel owners."

Sympathy for the woman's loss spread through Willow's chest. The murders of Stacey and her boyfriend, Jonas Digby, in Mount Rainier National Park had shocked all the Stark Lodge employees.

And Mara Gilmore, who not only had a motive but would have had access to the PNK9-issued murder weapon, had been spotted fleeing the scene.

Where are you, Mara? Willow silently wondered, wishing her friend would turn herself in so they could clear her name and shift the investigation to hunting the real killer.

Janet continued, "Well, the remaining owner and the lodge manager."

"Eli Ballard is the remaining owner, correct?" Willow asked, recalling the latest briefing on the case by Chief Fanelli. Stacey's brother would soon inherit her half of the business, but he had immediately been cleared as a suspect and was now engaged to PNK9 officer Danica Hayes.

"Yes, ma'am," Janet said. "He's in his office. At least, he was last time I saw him." She pointed down a corridor behind the desk.

"We need to speak to him," Theo informed her.

"Of course." Janet motioned for them to follow her around the reception desk and to the Employees Only door. "Mr. Ballard's office is at the end of the hall."

Willow pushed through the door, letting Star take the lead. The dog sniffed the air and the ground but didn't alert. To the right was a conference room with an oval table and several chairs. The light was off and the room empty.

They moved past the lodge manager's office. Through the glass window they could see the lights were off in the room and it was empty, as well. They proceeded farther down the corridor, past an open lunchroom with refrigerators, microwaves, a sink and three round tables and chairs. At the end of the hall, there were two doors, both closed. To the left, a placard on the door read Stacey Stark. The windows into the office had the blinds shut.

On the door to the right, a placard read Eli Ballard. The door was closed, and the blinds were also shut. Someone, undoubtedly Eli, had written on the whiteboard that hung on the door in black marker, *Visiting the North Cascades Stark Lodge. Returning tomorrow.*

Theo turned the doorknob. Locked.

Frustration beat a sharp tempo behind Willow's eyes.

"Seems no one's in charge today," Theo

said, his voice laced with a mocking cynicism that grated on Willow's nerves.

He never used to be so sarcastic. What happened to him? She wanted to ask him, to delve into why he'd changed, but she'd been down that path already and had been shut down. Shut out. And now it was too late. She really had to learn to compartmentalize. A feat she just wasn't good at.

They went back to the reception desk.

"Where's the lodge manager?" Theo asked.

"He called in sick today. Hopefully, he'll be back tomorrow. Is Mr. Ballard not in his office?"

"He is not." Theo looked back toward the stairwell and the locked door. "You don't have access to the keys for that door?"

"I'm afraid not."

"Do you have a way to reach Mr. Ballard?" Willow asked.

"I have his cell phone number," Janet replied. She fished around the reception desk until she found one of Eli's business cards and handed it to Willow.

Taking out her cell phone, Willow dialed the number listed on the card. After a moment, Eli's voice mail picked up. Grinding her teeth, Willow waited for the beep then said into the phone, "Mr. Ballard, this is Officer Willow

Bates with the Pacific Northwest K-9 Unit. It's imperative that I speak with you. I'm at the Stark Lodge near Olympic National Park. Please, call me at this number." Willow gave her cell phone number. She hung up and looked at Theo. "Now we wait."

Theo grunted an agreement and headed for the elevator with their bags.

Willow's hand tightened around Star's leash as they approached the elevator. They stepped into the elevator, and the door closed. Willow found the small box uncomfortable as she and Theo stood shoulder to shoulder. At one time she would have slipped her hand into his.

If only there was a way to travel back in time to when things between them hadn't been turned upside down. But time travel wasn't possible, and the reality was they were strangers now.

She shoved her hands inside the pockets of her jacket.

They stepped out on the top floor. The placard on the door at the end of the hall read Presidential Suite. Theo slid the key card across the sensor, opening the lock. He pushed the door open and stepped aside for Willow and Star to enter. The gentlemanly gesture shouldn't have surprised her. He'd always had good manners.

The suite was spacious indeed. A wall of

windows with a sliding glass door leading to a balcony overlooking the backside of the property provided lots of natural light. A kitchenette on the other side of a granite counter held a microwave, a small refrigerator and a coffee infuser machine with a stand filled with a variety of flavored pods. A large table and chairs took up space to the left, while a spacious living room with a couch and giant-screen TV took up the rest of the common area. At opposite ends of the suite were closed doors.

Theo moved to the sliding glass door and stared out at the view. "Take your pick."

Staring at his back, she pushed away the sad thought that he couldn't even look at her. She and Star pivoted left and took the room farthest from the main door. She unleashed Star so the dog could become acquainted with their surroundings. The bedroom had a king-size bed, a desk, a large-screen TV and en suite bath with a Jacuzzi tub. The room had its own balcony with comfy-looking chairs and a small table. She opened the slider and stepped out, breathing in the fresh pine-scented air.

The view was breathtaking. Tall old-growth pines and firs ringed a beautiful lawn with three fire pits circled by garden chairs. Closer to the hotel there was a patio with tables and chairs underneath wide umbrellas. The coverage wasn't for the sun but for the inevitable Pacific Northwest rain.

This was a good choice. Much better than being cooped up with Theo in a home full of memories. She wasn't sure her heart could take the agony of having Theo underfoot but yet so far away emotionally.

"I'm starving," Theo said from the doorway to the room.

Willow turned to face him, drinking in the way he leaned against the doorjamb, lean and muscled. Thinner than when they'd met. His cheeks had hollowed out and his eyes held a haunted expression at the edges, making her wish there was some way to comfort him. But those days were long gone. He'd rejected her attempts at soothing whatever tormented him. The sting still resonated through her, creating ripples of hurt.

Quelling the riot of emotions inside her, she assessed her hunger. She wasn't famished or anything, but she needed to keep up her strength, for the baby's sake. "I could eat."

Star slipped past Theo to explore the rest of the suite.

He held up a menu. "Room service? Or dining room?"

Feeling fatigued from the day's events and

her shoulder throbbed, Willow said, "Room service. Burgers on the menu?"

"I believe so." Theo read the menu and grinned. "Charbroiled burger, Gorgonzola cheese, sautéed mushrooms and onion rings, tomatoes, lettuce."

In response to the mouthwatering ingredients, her stomach rumbled. Okay, maybe a bit famished after all. She'd noticed her eating habits had increased in volume and regularity since being pregnant. The books she'd read assured her it was normal. Eating for two and all that. "Yes, please."

The slight smile curving his lips sent her pulse jumping.

"Fries? Or salad?"

Unable to look away from him, she said, "One of each."

His chuckle filled the space between them. How long had it been since she'd heard him laugh? A year. Ever since he'd changed.

"Share?"

His question, though innocent enough, slammed into her chest like a fist. She wouldn't have thought twice about sharing a food order with him in the past. But now, even that simple activity seemed too intimate. It would be bad enough dining together in the same room. She eyed the desk situated in the corner. "No. And I think I'll eat in this room."

Theo's expression blanked. He gave a sharp nod and retreated, shutting the door behind him. Moments later there was a scratch on the door.

Willow opened the door, allowing Star back in. "I'm sure you're hungry, too."

Moving into the common space, Willow was almost relieved to see that Theo had disappeared behind the closed door of the other bedroom. She hadn't hurt his feelings, had she? She didn't know. He used to be so easy to read. But then… She shook her head. She didn't know him anymore. Being with him was like starting over. Did she want to know him again? Where would it lead? To more heartbreak?

No, thank you.

Yet, they had a child on the way. They were going to be parents. How that would work, she wasn't sure. Something to figure out on another day. They had time.

Star nudged her as if to hurry her along.

Willow made the hand movement for sit. Star obeyed, her tail thumping against the carpeted floor.

"Stay."

Moving to where Theo had put Star's food

on the kitchen counter, Willow put her hand on her abdomen. For the baby's sake, she supposed she needed to find some way of reaching a middle ground with Theo. She needed to ask him if he even wanted to be included in their child's life. She wanted him to be involved. A child needed their father. The grief of losing her own stabbed at her, familiar and dreaded.

Theo's innate sense of fairness and justice had always been a draw to her. She'd appreciated his willingness to listen and to advise when needed. He'd make a great father.

Or at least the man she'd once fallen in love with would have made a great father. She didn't know the man he'd become.

But she didn't need to have him in their lives if he didn't want to be. Forcing him would only end up hurting them all.

The thought of raising her child alone brought the sudden prick of tears, burning the backs of her eyes. She remembered how hard it had been on her mom after her father's death. The struggle to makes ends meet before the insurance money kicked in, and even then, they'd lived month to month. Her mom always worrying about money and resources for Willow and her brother, Benton.

Willow and Benton had pitched in as best they could through their teen years. Benton had joined the air force right out of high school and was now stationed overseas. Willow had gone to the junior college and received a criminal justice degree, which dovetailed nicely into the police academy. She hoped her father would be proud of her. It hurt to know her child would never know their grandfather.

Shaking off the melancholy and the despair seeping into her consciousness, she concentrated on taking care of Star.

After putting water in a bowl and setting the food bowl on the floor, she released Star from her sit. While the dog ate, Willow took her bags into her room and unpacked her clothes. Three fresh uniforms, yoga pants and tops, one casual dress, and a pair of sandals she'd thrown in at the last second, along with her running shoes and hiking boots. She didn't anticipate they would be here long, but she liked things to be neat and orderly.

Another thing she and Theo had always shared. Organizational skills abounded between them. They'd loved to geek out over spreadsheets and thoughtfully arranged cupboards.

Willow blew out a breath. Why couldn't she have a thought without making it about Theo?

She grabbed Star's leash and headed back out to the living space. Star was done eating and was staring out the slider to the living room's balcony. Willow attached the lead to Star's collar. She raised her hand to knock on Theo's door, but the door opened before she could make contact with the wood.

She stepped back as Theo stepped forward, his scent wrapping around her like a fuzzy blanket.

Suddenly unable to breathe properly, she managed to squeeze past the lump in her throat, "I'm taking Star out. She just ate." Theo would understand this was part of their routine. Structure was good. Keeping to a schedule brought order and focus into her world. Theo's world, too, at one time. Did it still?

His dark, observant eyes searched her face. "Want company?"

It took all her willpower not to say yes. How many times had she longed for his presence? Longed for him to be at her side? But he'd stayed away. Volunteering for more undercover assignments. Why? What had she done? What happened to him?

Hardening her resolve to maintain distance, she said, "Someone should stay in case the food arrives."

He gave her a crooked grin. Her heart flip-flopped.

"Of course," he said. "I can take her out.

You've had a hard day." He reached for the leash. "You should be resting."

She held on to the leash, resentment coming swiftly. She didn't want him telling her what to do, regardless of whether his statement was true. He'd lost the privilege to be concerned over her well-being when he'd left. "Not necessary."

His fingers curled over hers, setting off an electric spark that traveled up her arm and exploded somewhere in the vicinity of her heart.

"I insist," Theo said.

"I resist," Willow stated with a good dose of hostility in her tone. She was acting childish, but she couldn't seem to help it. This man brought out the best and the worst her in. Always had.

Star's head bobbed between her two people. She nudged Willow with her nose, then moved to stand next to Theo, causing the lead to stretch away from Willow.

"Traitor." Sometimes Willow was sure Star understood English. She was choosing Theo to take her out. Because she missed him? Or because she agreed that Willow needed to rest?

She really did need to take a breather if she was assigning human motives to Star.

With a sigh of resignation, Willow released

her hold on the leash, along with the animosity crowding her chest.

Theo had the grace to not gloat. Instead, the soft smile in his eyes made her knees tremble.

"We'll be right back."

He and Star left through the suite door. It locked automatically behind them. But to be safe, she threw the bolt. Her boss's words about the bomber knowing who she was rang clear in her head. Though she doubted very much the assailant was keeping tabs on her. Why would he, or she?

Willow couldn't identify the person who'd pushed her, nor could she say it was the same person who set off the explosive at the trail marker.

She sank down on the couch with a sigh born of weariness and reprieve. Putting her feet up on the coffee table, she decided being overly cautious wouldn't hurt.

She leaned her head back and closed her eyes. It seemed no time at all had passed before she heard a knock at the suite's door. Rousing, she made her way to the door and looked through the peephole. A young man with a service cart stood there waiting. Willow's hand went to the bolt, but a sudden spike of fear had her hesitating. Maybe she should wait for Theo?

She shook her head at her own paranoia. She was a trained officer, able to handle herself. No reason to act like a ninny. She opened the door.

The kid couldn't have been more than twenty. He wore a white shirt, black vest and black slacks. "Room service for Bates?"

The ding of the elevator and the swoosh of the doors opening down the hall had Willow tensing, but then Star and Theo stepped out, and she was surprised by the wave of relief washing over her. She stepped back, allowing the young man to push the cart into the room. She realized she had no money on her to tip him with.

"I've got it," Theo said as he and Star stopped just outside the door.

Was she still so easy to read? The disconcerting thought made her uneasy. It wasn't fair that Theo should have the upper hand when it came to knowing her. But then again, nothing in life was ever truly fair. God never promised it would be.

The young man pivoted and took the bills Theo offered him. "Thanks, man. Very generous."

Theo waited until the hotel worker was in the elevator and the doors slid shut before he closed the suite door and let Star off her leash. Willow's stomach rumbled as the most heavenly scents rose from beneath silver domes. A bottle of sparkling apple cider sat in a bucket of ice. She lifted the bottle and noted that it was cranberry-flavored. Her favorite. Unsure what to make of the sweet gesture, her gaze jumped to Theo. Should she be happy that he'd remembered? Or upset that he'd remembered?

Her emotions were flustered, and hunger suddenly tightened her belly.

He gave a half shrug. "I figured we should at least toast to the baby."

She swallowed down the rising uncertainties and forced herself to say, "Maybe we should wait until I'm past the first trimester."

His brow creased. Alarm deepened the dark depths of his eyes. "Are you worried?"

"No," she was quick to assure him. She couldn't be intentionally cruel, not even to someone who had ripped her heart to shreds. "The doctor said everything is fine, and the likelihood of a miscarriage goes down once the second trimester is reached, which is soon, but still…"

He visibly exhaled, as if he'd held his breath while waiting for her answer. "I can understand the concern. But I want to celebrate every milestone. Learning we're going to be parents is big."

The earnestness of his voice wrapped around

her, cocooning her in a pleasurable glow. She stared at him, her mouth going dry. Was that his subtle way of saying he wanted to be involved in their child's life? In her life?

Why did the thought fill her with joy?

No. Wait. Not her life. The baby's.

She refused to open herself up to that kind of hurt again. Theo had the power to destroy her. She wouldn't allow that. Couldn't allow it. She needed to stay strong for the baby. "Fine."

She lifted the dome off one of the plates. A juicy hamburger held together by a large toothpick beckoned, along with a pile of fries and a salad with the ranch dressing on the side. As Theo popped the cap off the bottle of sparkling cranberry cider and poured two glasses, she picked up a fry and dipped it in the ranch dressing. Hunger pains cramped in her stomach. Suddenly ravenous, she wanted to dive into her meal, but she held herself in check and took the glass he held out. They clinked the rims together.

"To a new life," he said.

He couldn't know how true those words were.

"To a new life," she repeated.

Not only to the life growing inside her, but to the new lives they would have going forward. Separately.

She took a quick sip, letting the cool bubbles

slide down her throat. It would be too easy to fall back into old patterns. To play the role of wife, a role she'd enjoyed and had never expected to surrender. Deep heartache wound through her, making her want to gnash her teeth and throw something at the wall. Time to retreat away from the source of her anguish.

"Good night, Theo." She lifted the tray with her free hand and headed to her room, where she set the tray on the desk. Aware that Star hadn't followed her, she stood in the doorway to find Star had jumped up on the couch and made herself comfortable on the throw pillows.

Willow met Theo's gaze across the room. He held his tray in his hands. He offered a slight smile. "I think she'll be okay."

"I'll leave my door cracked open for her," Willow said.

"So will I."

She wanted to tell him not to bother. Star was her partner. But they both had raised her. Leaving the door cracked open, Willow hurried back to her food. Her mouth watered, but anxiety made the thought of eating unpalatable. Her conscience pricked her. Nourishing the baby was important, and that meant she would eat even if she was upset. She bowed her head and lifted a prayer for protection and thanksgiving for the food.

Deep inside she knew she was going through the motions. But the verse in the Bible about faith as small as a mustard seed rose to her mind. She did have faith. Just not in herself or her marriage.

Theo checked and double-checked the slider in the living room and the suite's main door. He stopped before Willow's door, staying out of the line of sight through the narrow opening, and listened to see if there was any sign of distress. He hoped she'd remembered to lock her sliding glass door.

Ugh. He paced away. Of course she would. She was a smart, capable woman who didn't need him. She'd never needed him. But he'd needed her. Still did in some ways. But there was too much water under the bridge. Too much regret and too much guilt to ever think they could recapture their former life together.

He stopped in front of the slider to stare up at the night sky, where rain clouds drifted, allowing the bright moon to peek through, seeming to mock him. So beautiful, perfectly round. A full moon. His gaze dropped to the tree line and down to the ground, where shadows shifted in the slight breeze. The windows were shut, but he could almost hear the patter of rain falling through the pines and hemlock.

Washington in June was always wet. With the occasional sunny days to tease visitors into a false sense of hope that the rain they'd heard about in the Pacific Northwest wasn't really true.

He'd missed the rain. Right now, Washington, DC, was hot and muggy already, with the summer predicted to be a scorcher.

Rubbing the back of his neck, he acknowledged the fatigue of flying halfway across the country was starting to wear on him. He needed to rest. Because he had to be alert tomorrow.

Finding the person responsible for bombing the forest was of paramount importance. More importantly, he had to keep Willow safe. But could he protect their hearts?

FIVE

The next morning, Theo was up with the sunrise, showered, dressed and making coffee by the time Willow emerged from her room carrying a small backpack. She wore a fresh uniform of forest green slacks and matching long-sleeve shirt. A patch on the shirt's front left pocket bore the PNK9 Unit logo. She'd pulled her long brown hair into a low ponytail. Her face was devoid of makeup, but he knew she wore a moisturizer with sunscreen every day. She'd convinced him to start doing the same, saying even during cloud cover, the sun's rays penetrated through the gloom and trees to wreak havoc on the skin.

The memory held a sharp sting. A memory of a better time.

Theo's gaze lingered on her face. Her beautiful blue eyes had attracted him on the first day they'd met. She'd looked at him much as she was now, with so much intensity that he was afraid she could see all the way to his soul. Back then, he'd relished truly being seen. Now, the shame and guilt inside him squirmed beneath her perusal.

Her gaze raked over him, as intimate as a touch. He'd changed out of his FBI persona, the suit and tie, and into everyday wear. Jeans, waterproof shoes and a lightweight, button-down shirt that would wick the moisture from his body.

Star darted straight to the sliding glass door and scratched.

"I'll take her out," Theo told Willow. He needed fresh air to get his head on straight. He couldn't let down his guard. He refused to burden Willow with his disgrace. "I made a pot of coffee."

His FBI rain slicker was draped across the back of the couch. He shrugged into it and picked up Star's leash from the counter.

"Thank you for the coffee," Willow said. "But these days, I'm into peppermint tea. Helps the nausea."

He grimaced. He should have remembered—no caffeine for a pregnant woman. And he wouldn't own up to the lapse, because he feared she'd take offense. But he'd only learned of the pregnancy yesterday. It was something he was going to have to get used to. They had a child on the way. His mind still grappled to comprehend it. "There's a hot water spigot next to the faucet."

With a nod, Willow picked up the mug he had set out for her and filled it with hot water. Then, from the pocket of her backpack, she pulled out a foil-wrapped tea bag. He watched her slender, capable fingers rip open the top and slip out the silky tea bag. He stood there, mesmerized, as she dipped the tea bag in the water while holding on to the little string. He loved her grace and fluidity. Always had. She froze.

Her gaze jumped to his, as if she'd suddenly become aware of his eyes on her. Embarrassed to be caught staring and really hoping the longing for closeness filling his chest wasn't visible in his expression, he quickly leashed Star and left the hotel room, making sure the door closed completely.

In the parking lot of the Stark Lodge, Theo noted two PNK9 vehicles parked next to his borrowed one.

Jackson must be here, along with more team members.

After letting Star have time in the trees, Theo led the dog back to the presidential suite on the third floor. Inside, just as he suspected, he found Jackson Dean, along with four other young officers, two of whom Theo had met the day before.

Willow stepped forward to take Star's lead. "Theo, you remember Jackson and the two candidates, Veronica and Owen, who'll be shadowing him."

Theo nodded his head at the two.

Then Willow gestured to the other two people standing there looking at him curiously. "This is Officer Brandie Weller and Officer Parker Walsh. They're the other two candidates and will be shadowing us. This is my— This is Theo Bates with the FBI."

Theo's stomach clenched at her hesitation to claim him as her husband. Another thing he was going to have to get used to. "Nice to meet you both. Glad to have the extra sets of eyes."

Jackson's blue gaze went from Willow to Theo. The speculative gleam made Theo wonder if Willow had mentioned their recent estrangement and the baby. "We'll be hitting the coastline."

Willow nodded. "I'm going to show Theo where the blast was yesterday."

"Good idea," Jackson said. "I'm sure you'll be able to help us figure out who is targeting our trails and why."

"I'm certainly going to try," Theo assured him. "And keep my—Willow—safe."

Theo ignored Willow's frown. No doubt she wanted to deny she needed protecting.

"Willow has spoken often of your ability to assess situations and bring to light information that others might miss," Jackson said.

A skill that could have taken Theo in a different direction. He'd chosen undercover work, where assessing lies, deception and manipulation meant life or death at any given moment.

Looking to Willow, Theo said, "We should track down Eli Ballard, as well."

"I called him again while you and Star were out," Willow told him. "He'll be back later this afternoon. He wasn't happy to cut his plans short."

Theo wasn't surprised she'd made the call. Willow was a hard worker and industrious. The type of person who didn't let the grass grow under her feet. Another one of the many things he had enjoyed about her. Their downtime had always included some sort of adventure, whether it was parasailing in the ocean, hiking or kayaking. He missed those days. When they were young and carefree and in love.

Those days were long gone now. He turned away from Willow. He didn't even recognize the person he was back then. He was not the same man. It would be way too much to ask her to forgive him. Way too much for him to seek forgiveness.

"I'll grab the keys." He went into his room and inhaled several deep breaths, squared his shoulders and fortified the walls around his heart. His mission here was to protect Willow and find a bomber. To complete that mission, he needed to stay professional.

An easy thing to say but harder to do.

Theo brought the SUV to a halt at the parking area for the rain forest trail. Willow's heart thumped. Had it only been yesterday when she and Star had been on the trail, had found a bomb and been pushed at the exact moment of the explosion? It seemed as if time had sped up since then.

She glanced at Theo as he turned off the engine.

Somehow, time also seemed to have slowed.

Theo sat with his hands on the steering wheel staring straight ahead. Worry lines bracketed his eyes. She wanted to know what he was thinking. There had been a time when they would've shared every thought and emotion. But that was before. Before he'd shut her out and left her so easily. Resentment and sadness burned at the backs of her eyes.

Frustrated at herself for the stir of emotions, she popped open her door and climbed out. Another SUV pulled up next to them. Parker and Brandie. Willow released Star from the special compartment and walked to the edge of the trail, letting Star sniff around. The two candidates held on to their German shepherds.

Theo gestured to Willow. "Lead the way."

With a nod, she gave a slight tug on Star's lead, then headed out. Theo stayed close to her, his presence steadying the nerves ricocheting through her. The two hopefuls hung back a bit, and Willow could hear the pair murmuring. When they reached a bend in the trail, Star's nose went to the air. The dog pulled at her lead, forcing them at a quicker pace.

"Is she alerting?" Parker asked, a thread of excitement in his tone. "Do you think it's another bomb?"

"Let's hope not," Brandie said, dread lacing her words.

Though all four contenders for the two open slots with the unit were K-9 officers, they were generalists and didn't yet specialize the way the PNK9 officers did.

Willow made a mental note of the two candidates' very different reactions. She studied

Parker a moment. Veronica claimed it was Parker who moved her weapon and badge, but the man denies it. Would he purposely do something to hurt the other candidates?

Theo touched Willow's arm, drawing her attention. "Are you sure you're up for this?"

She shook off his hand and sent him a glare. "I've already told you, I'm fine. Now, quiet, everyone. Let us work."

Willow let Star lead the way. The dirt trail showed signs of use—lots of footprints and scuffs. Ahead of them, the burned remains of the trail marker loomed. Darkened earth created by the blast formed a semicircular indentation in the ground. The crime scene tape that had been strung across the path now lay in the dirt, and three Olympic National Park rangers, dressed in the standard forest green uniform, were busy cleaning up the mess left by the explosion. One held a rake and was sifting the earth, trying to smooth out the terrain. Another picked up debris, piling it off to the side. The third inspected the vegetation, cutting back burned edges of the foliage, no doubt to preserve the plants.

"Good morning," Willow called out.

Two of the rangers hurried to meet them. The third hung back, continuing to rake the dirt and fill in the crater left by the blast.

One of the rangers, a stocky guy with dark hair and eyes, held up a hand. "Sorry, but this trail is closed."

Willow smiled, hoping to put the rangers at ease. "We're with the Pacific Northwest K-9 unit. I'm Officer Willow Bates, and this is my partner, Star. We were the ones that found the explosive device."

The other ranger stepped forward and stuck out her hand. She was at least six feet tall with wavy golden hair tied back at her nape. "I'm Kathleen, this is Mitch and—" she gestured over her shoulder "—that's Chaz."

Willow accepted the offered hand. "Thank you, Kathleen. I appreciate the work you all are doing."

"We were glad to hear you weren't hurt, Willow," Kathleen stated.

"She was hurt," Theo fairly snapped. "She took shrapnel in her shoulder. I'm surprised the crime scene has been released already."

Shooting Theo a censuring glare, Willow said, "A small piece of debris."

"The crime scene techs were here all day yesterday and earlier this morning. They only released this area an hour or so ago," Mitch said.

Star sniffed at the two rangers' booted feet, then sat and let out a series of barks.

"She's alerting on the bomb residue you have tracked onto yourselves," Willow explained.

"Makes sense," Kathleen said. "It's going to take a bit for us to get this all cleared away."

"When will a new trailhead marker go in?" Parker asked, stepping up.

"We put in a request for one," Mitch said.

"It could take weeks," Kathleen said.

Willow dug into her backpack and brought out three business cards. She handed one to Kathleen and Mitch. Then she and Star moved closer to the burned-out trailhead, where she handed a card to Chaz.

"Please, call me if you see or hear anything that might help us find who did this," she said.

Without looking at her, Chaz took the small white card and stuck it in the pocket of his shirt.

"You mind if we take a look?" Willow asked him.

The man shrugged and stepped away, moving to where three backpacks sat on the ground. He hunched down to retrieve a water bottle. Willow inspected the charred remains of the trail marker.

Theo joined her. He pointed to a spot on the post that seemed darker than the rest of the trailhead marker. "Ignition point?"

"Most likely the explosive device was attached here." Willow had seen the aftermath of enough explosions to confidently make such a statement. "It had enough force pointed downward to create the crater around the post. Whoever set this wanted the ground to take most of the blast."

"I would love to know how I can get involved with the K-9 unit," Kathleen said.

"It's an elite group," Parker said, earning himself an elbow nudge from Brandie. "What? It's true."

Brandie rolled her eyes. "You can find an application on the state's website. It is true that K-9 officers go through a very rigorous training, and PNK9 training takes it a step further, since they're assigned to the national parks."

"But we are always looking for new recruits," Willow said then turned her attention to Theo. "I'd like to see where the person who pushed me went."

Theo nodded. "Good idea."

Keeping a close eye on the dog for any sign of alerting to more explosive devices, Willow led Star through the thick underbrush. Theo and the two candidates and their two dogs followed. Mist hung in the air, dampening their clothing as they went deeper into the forest. Tree limbs scratched and snagged at their pant legs and the sleeves of their shirts. Ten minutes later, they came out onto a gravel fire road.

Which direction? Willow shielded her eyes against the midmorning sun. "Left would lead back to the main road."

"The suspect could've had a car waiting," Theo offered.

"True." Willow gave Star the search command, knowing if there were any trace amounts of the explosive material used to make the bomb lingering in the air or on the ground, Star would find them and follow the trail. The dog went to work, sniffing the ground, but instead of going to the left toward the main road, she turned to the right, following the fire road.

Not knowing where the road would lead or how far the scent trail would take them, Willow's nerves stretched taut. "Here we go." She started off, and when Theo made the move to fall into step beside her, Willow called out, "Brandie, walk with me."

Theo watched Willow walk ahead of him with Brandie. He shouldn't be surprised that his wife—soon-to-be ex-wife—was using the candidate as a buffer. Having seen the destruction of the trail marker and knowing how close Willow had come to being seriously injured cramped Theo's chest. If she had been any closer to that marker, she would have ended up with more than just debris in her shoulder. Willow and their child could have been seriously hurt. Was the person who pushed Willow the same person who set off the bomb? If not the bomber, then why push Willow? Or was that person out in the woods doing something else illegal they didn't want anybody to know about?

"So, you're with the FBI," Parker said as he and his German shepherd joined Theo. "I thought about joining the FBI."

"It's not for everyone," Theo murmured.

"Oh, I'd have been a great FBI agent," Parker said, his voice filled with confidence. "I'm a good investigator."

Theo shot a glance at the younger man. "But you decided to be a K-9 officer."

"That's right. Rosie and I work well together." Parker indicated the beautiful German shepherd walking at his side. Rosie's dark eyes stared up at Theo as if she realized they were talking about her.

Theo smiled at the dog. "She's well trained."

Knowing how much training went into the dogs of the Pacific Northwest K-9 Unit, Theo was always impressed. In fact, all the law enforcement agencies that had K-9s on board went through very demanding and ongoing training to make sure that the dog and handler were bonded, as well as in sync with one another. Making sure dogs obeyed out in the field had to be a certainty. The handler needed to know they could count on the dog. And the dog had to know they could count on the handler. Theo knew this from all the time and training that had been given to Star. He'd always admired Willow's dedication.

"We do extra training," Parker said with a dash of pride. "I'm doing everything I can to secure a position with the unit."

"If you pay attention to Willow, you'll learn a lot."

"It's pretty cool you get to work with your wife," Parker commented. "That would be something, to work with the woman you love every day."

A deep ache forced breath from Theo's lungs. "I'm only here temporarily, helping to find the serial bomber. Then I head back to DC."

"DC can't compare to the Pacific Northwest," the younger man said. "I'm from one of the best small towns in the whole state of Washington. I was the department's first K-9 officer." Parker's chest puffed up a bit. "And I cracked a murder case nobody else could figure out. It was pretty awesome, if I say so myself."

Theo suppressed a grimace at the other man's bragging. As Parker launched into his tale of heroics, Theo bit back a sigh. It was going to be a long walk. He kept his gaze on Willow. As long as nothing happened to her, Theo could endure anything.

SIX

Willow hated to admit how devastating it had been to visit the burned-out trailhead marker. Especially under Theo's scrutiny. Seeing the charred remains brought back horrible memories, vaulting her mind to that day long ago when her father had taken her to the park because she wanted to go hiking.

She remembered her father walking up to the kiosk, then a man delaying him while she'd waited impatiently as only a thirteen-year-old girl could. She'd climbed out of the car and had been about to prompt her father to hurry when he'd broken away from the man and stepped up to the pay machine. Seconds later, an explosion had taken out the kiosk. Willow had been thrown to the ground. When she'd recovered enough to sit up, all she could see was smoke and debris.

And her father and the other man lying on the ground.

Willow's thoughts were forced to the present when Brandie said with a huff, "There he goes again."

Willow shot the young candidate a glance. "Who? What?"

Star lifted her nose in the air and then back to the ground, staying on a straight course while Brandie's German shepherd zigged and zagged as they continued down the gravel fire road.

"Parker." Brandie's voice lowered. "He's always bragging. We all know he solved a murder case. He's told us enough times."

Glancing over her shoulder, Willow met Theo's gaze as he listened to Parker's tale. Her soon-to-be ex-husband's eyebrows rose and his lips twisted in a wry smile. Obviously, he wasn't exactly finding Parker riveting. Forcing her attention to the woman at her side, Willow asked, "Have you and Parker been paired often?"

"Off and on. Chief Fanelli rotates us around. We've shadowed different officers. He's also had us working on the Mara Gilmore case."

Willow's heart contracted in her chest. The thought of her friend out there, on the run, accused of murder—a crime Willow did not believe Mara had committed—hurt Willow's heart. Unfortunately, Willow had no proof

Mara wasn't guilty, just as there was nothing but circumstantial evidence suggesting that Mara was the murderer.

Maybe Brandie had new information Willow had missed while she was dealing with the bombing case. "What have you learned so far?"

"It's so complicated, with so many moving parts," Brandie said. "But I'm sure the team will crack it and bring Mara home. Bring her to justice."

Willow frowned, not liking the suggestion that Brandie thought Mara was guilty. "There's nothing concrete to go on, correct?"

"Other than two PNK9 officers seeing Mara fleeing the scene? And a unit-issued gun found…?" Brandie paused. "Of course, you know that part, since you and Star found the weapon."

"Just to be clear, there were no fingerprints on the gun," Willow stated firmly.

"Right. But the assumption—"

Willow cut the woman off. "I do not believe Mara Gilmore is guilty of the charges against her."

Brandie's eyes widened slightly. "Good to know. If she isn't, I think it's so unfair that Mara should be forced to live a life she didn't choose, that criminal people chose for her—"

Willow tucked in her chin in surprise. "What criminal people are you talking about?"

"Well, isn't it obvious? Somebody is making her do what she's doing." Brandie shrugged. "I mean, there has to be a reason she is running from the police. If she's not guilty, then the only other option is somebody must be forcing her into hiding."

Swallowing back the rise of anxiety, Willow had to admit she agreed with the young candidate. Was Mara's life in danger? Had someone threatened her? Had she seen the real killer? What had her so scared that she wouldn't trust her friends? Or even her brother, Asher?

Brandie shielded her eyes against the sun. "People do things because they're forced to all the time. Things they wouldn't do if they had any other choice."

Willow studied the young woman. Her passionate words rang true, as if she was speaking from personal experience. Had someone forced Brandie to do something against her will? "I'm a really good listener, Brandie, if you want to—"

Brandie moved away and pointed. "Hey, we're at the ranger station."

Up ahead, the station came into view amid the trees. The box-shaped building had been painted brown to blend in with the surrounding forest. A small porch with an overhang provided cover for the front door. An American flag hung from a tall pole. Parked out front was a white SUV with the words *US Park Ranger* in green across the side.

Brandie picked up her pace with her dog, Taz, a beautiful German shepherd, clearly eager to work.

Willow waited for Theo to catch up to her. Parker paused, briefly looking at both of them, and then hurried after Brandie.

"I'm going to let Star sniff around the outside and see if we can pick up the scent again moving away from the ranger station. I find it hard to believe whoever pushed me went inside."

Theo gestured for her to move forward. In a different time, she would have taken the opportunity to put her hand on his arm or to pass by and lean in for a kiss. Those days were gone.

Pushing back the sadness that lurked at the edges of her mind, she gave Star the search command. Star led them straight to the door of the ranger station, where Parker and Brandie both waited.

"I thought we should go in, but—" Parker pointed to Brandie. "She thought we needed to wait for you."

"Star says our bomber went in here," Willow said. "Waiting was the better choice." Good on Brandie for her levelheadedness, and good on Parker for heeding the caution. It was important that the team listen to each other and work together.

Theo turned to the two candidates. "Take a walk around the building. See if there's another access point or another path leading away from here. Keep an eye on the ground for footprints."

"We can do that, agent man," Parker said with a salute. He and Rosie headed around the building.

Brandie shook her head and hurried after him.

Willow suppressed a smile at Parker's use of *agent man*. She waited to see how Theo would react. He pushed open the ranger station door without a word. Surprise washed over her. It seemed he'd matured since the last time somebody called him *agent man*.

Inside the station they found a park ranger studying a map. There were several survey records spread out across the expanse of the table before him.

Dressed in a khaki uniform, with sandy hair that was turning gray, the park ranger frowned, creating wrinkles on his weathered face. He straightened and studied them. "Can I help you?"

Willow introduced herself and Theo.

"I'm Steve Adkins. What is this about?"

"We're here investigating the recent bombings," Theo told him.

Steve gave a grave nod. "Nasty business, that. I've been trying to figure out why someone would set off explosive devices in my forest."

"You have a theory?" Willow asked, her gaze straying to the map with the dots running across the center of the Olympic National Forest. She moved closer, hoping to catch a glimpse of the survey records. Was there a problem with the forest? Something their suspect was trying to cover up? Was this park ranger involved?

Star paid the man no heed.

"I think I do," Steve said. "There's an action-adventure group lobbying the state to put in an all-terrain vehicle trail running from here..." Steve pointed on the map and trailed his finger along several dots until he came to the last dot, located on the exact opposite side of the park. "To here. The two trailhead markers that were destroyed are on this line."

Willow's breath caught in her throat. Her

gaze sought Theo's. He gave a nod—clearly his mind had gone in the same direction as hers.

Had they just discovered the motivation behind the bombings? Was an ecoterrorist group trying to thwart plans to put a motorized vehicle trail through the middle of the park? Were they bent on stopping the construction of the new off-road vehicle trail and didn't care who they hurt?

"Can you tell us who has visited this station in the past few days?" Willow asked.

"Most of the time this station isn't manned," Steve said. "I stopped in because I needed space to spread out." He gestured at the map and surveys.

"So there's no way to tell who came through here recently." Frustration threaded through Theo's voice, matching the feeling coursing through Willow.

"I'm afraid not. Sometimes people sign in, but mostly this is a place for hikers to grab a map or fill their water bottles," Steve explained. "Occasionally, a guided tour will stop in."

Willow took out her phone and photographed the map and the survey reports and sent them to Donovan. "This sort of trail would forever alter the park. I can't believe the Washington

State Parks and Recreation Commission would approve this."

Steve shrugged. "There are some very influential and powerful people lobbying for the trail."

"Thank you for your time," Theo said.

As they headed for the exit, Willow handed Steve her card. "We'll keep searching for the bomber."

"As will we," Steve said.

Outside the ranger station, Willow and Theo met up with Brandie and Parker. Willow filled them in on what they'd learned.

"That's not good," Parker said. "I don't blame people for being upset at the idea of cutting an ATV trail through the forest, but planting explosives in protest seems extreme."

"Fanatics usually are extreme," Brandie said.

A shudder of dread worked down Willow's spine. If they were on the right track, she had a horrible feeling the bomber wouldn't stop until the plans for the trail were scuttled.

"I need to relay this information to my boss," Theo told Willow as they left the ranger station, heading back to where they'd left their vehicles. "This action-adventure group might have some ideas of who would be trying to shut them down." He walked ahead to make his call.

Images of the charred trail marker battered

at Willow's mind and crimped her heart. By the time they returned to the Stark Lodge, Willow had a splitting headache. Afraid she'd let herself get too dehydrated, she pounded two bottles of water and paced the bedroom.

Star leaped onto the bed and watched.

Too keyed up to relax, Willow needed to get out of there. She needed breathing room. She needed to be out protecting the forest she loved so dearly.

Picking up Star's leash, she headed out the bedroom door. Star jumped off the bed and followed. The living room was empty. All was quiet. She considered knocking on Theo's door to let him know she was going out but decided she needed a break from him. His constant presence wreaked havoc on her emotions.

As she passed the counter separating the kitchen from the living space, she grabbed the park map that Ranger Steve had given them. Seeing the Stark Lodge logo on a notepad, she grabbed a pen and quickly jotted a note to Theo.

Taking Star out. Be back soon.

She didn't want him worrying unnecessarily. She wasn't heartless, after all. But she didn't want his company right now.

Theo stared at the note written in Willow's familiar curvy script. The words seemed innocuous enough, yet his heart dropped to his toes, making him very aware of how little control he had over Willow. He was at the mercy of her stubborn independence. The very things that once attracted him to her now terrified him.

How long had she been gone? He checked his watch.

When they'd returned to the lodge an hour ago after their visit to the bombing site at the trailhead and talking to the park ranger, they both had retreated to their rooms. He'd showered and changed, fully intending to ask Willow to join him for a late lunch so he could tell her about his conversation with his boss.

But she'd left. Unescorted.

He reminded himself she was a capable officer. Star might not be trained in apprehension or guard duty, but the dog would protect Willow if necessary.

Against a bomber? The thought sneaked through his brain like a thief, stealing any peace of mind he might have about letting Willow out of his sight. He tried to reassure himself with the thought that there was no reason to suspect the bomber would know Willow was staying at the lodge. No reason to believe she would be in danger on the grounds. If she stayed on the grounds.

She wouldn't go far. Would she?

Dread gripped him by the neck and squeezed.

Grabbing his jacket, he rushed out to find his errant wife.

Willow and Star made their way down a path behind the lodge. Off to the right, there was a large expanse of recently mowed green grass dotted with lawn games. Beyond that was a large patio with tables sporting umbrellas and chairs, filled with people. Obviously outdoor seating for the restaurant. A makeshift stage for live music had been constructed beneath a canopy. The scene was pretty and peaceful.

Veering to the left, she led Star on a footpath into the shadowed forest. As soon as they were out of sight of the lodge, she unleashed Star, letting the dog meander. It was good to allow her partner to be a dog. Even K-9s needed downtime.

The farther she and Star wandered, the deeper the shadows and the denser the foliage became. Late-afternoon sunlight barely penetrated the canopy of intertwined branches and leaves overhead. As Willow walked, she studied the map showing the line of the proposed new trail. With a start, she stopped in the middle of the path to glance around, then back at the map, and realized the entrance of the all-terrain vehicle trail would be off to her right toward Highway 101. Clicking her tongue into the roof of her mouth to draw Star's attention, she gestured for the pointer to follow her as Willow moved off the footpath and picked her way through the bushes. Star pushed past her to take the lead, occasionally looking over her shoulder to check in with Willow.

Keeping her gaze alert, Willow searched for signs of the new trail. Yellow Xs on a series of trees in a long line made her heart sink with dismay. These beautiful old-growth conifers and ancient flowering deciduous trees would be cut down to make way for the motorized vehicles.

The hairs on the back of Willow's neck rose, and her steps faltered. She had the strangest sensation she was being watched. She whirled to look behind her. No one was there. Star must have sensed Willow's agitation, because she moved to lean against her leg.

"Sorry, girl. I'm being paranoid," Willow muttered. To be cautious, she attached Star's leash to her collar.

Sweat gathered at Willow's nape as she and Star picked their way through the wild undergrowth and followed the line of trees that would eventually be demolished. They reached a clearing where the vegetation had been hacked away and a huge X had been spray-painted on the ground. This would be the entrance point. Off to her right, through the trees, she could see heavy construction equipment where they were making a new parking lot off the highway. Apparently, someone wasn't waiting for official approval.

To her left a twig snapped.

Willow's hand went to her sidearm, and she peered into the shadowed forest as dread sluiced through her veins. Star's tail was up and her ears were back.

"Willow?"

Theo's voice came from her right. Confused, Willow turned to find Theo standing at the edge of the clearing. His gaze bounced from her and Star to the dark canopy of woods where she'd heard the twig snapping.

More grateful than she dared admit, Willow rushed to Theo's side. "Something's out there."

"Or someone."

Theo's grave tone sent apprehension shuddering over her flesh, leaving her skin prickling.

He took her elbow, tugged her away from the clearing into the cover of the dense forest. "What were you doing out here by yourself? You shouldn't be alone. Next time you want to go out, you let me know."

She bristled, not wanting to confess how un-nerved she was now. "I left you a note. Besides, I don't need a babysitter."

"I think you do," he countered roughly. "We can't discount the ecoterrorist angle, nor the fact that the bomber doesn't seem to have any reservations about hurting people. And the perpetrator has seen you."

As if she could forget. "I hadn't meant to—"

From deep in the woods, a strange popping sound ricocheted off the trees. Birds squawked in protest.

Star barked and lunged on her leash toward the sound.

"She's alerting!" Willow's heart pounded in her throat.

Theo put his hand on his holstered weapon. "We need—"

A loud crack echoed across the forest, as loud as a gunshot blast. Shock jolted Willow's heart. She ducked, expecting bullets.

A cacophony of sound reverberated through the trees and buffeted against Willow like a tsunami.

"Watch out!"

Theo grabbed Willow, lifting her off her feet and running with her tucked against him like she was a football.

Star had no choice but to run alongside them

as Willow's hand clenched around the leash. Willow glanced back in time to see a huge, moss-covered old cedar drop through the trees.

Horror snatched her breath as the tree hit the ground. A shock wave of sound and energy propelled them forward, launching Theo off his feet. Incredibly, Theo adjusted Willow and twisted his body as he landed on his back, cradling Willow in his arms. Her head snapped back, hitting his shoulder. Bursts of light exploded behind her eyes. Star whined and hunched low to the ground.

She could only imagine the pain Theo had to be feeling from the whiplash and the weight of her crashing onto him.

There was no way the tree falling was an accident. If Theo hadn't reacted so swiftly...

She scrambled off Theo. His eyes were closed.

Terror knifed her heart. She touched his face. "Theo! Please let me know you're all right."

She gave him a small shake. Star licked his face.

He inhaled sharply.

Relief whooshed out of her lungs. Willow sat back on her heels and blinked back tears. He was alive.

Theo groaned as he rolled to his side and

then sat up. He rubbed the back of his head, his gaze locking with hers.

They stared at one another.

Something primeval arched between them. That was the only way she could explain why she reached for him. Her hands fisted around the collar of his windbreaker. She pulled him in close and kissed him on the mouth, so familiar yet so foreign.

His surprise was palpable in the stiffening of his body, and then his lips yielded. For a moment, all she wanted was to give in to the need for assurance that they were both alive and unharmed. But reality surfaced, a taunting reminder of the pain and heartache of loving Theo. Before she could indulge the sensations rocketing through her, she broke away and scrambled to her feet, her hand pressed over her heart. "That was close."

"Too close." Theo slowly made his way to his feet.

Willow saw the wince he tried to hide. She was at his side in seconds. The stitches in her shoulder pulled, but she ignored the momentary bite as she wrapped her arm around his waist. "Lean on me."

"I'm supposed to be saying that to you," he muttered, but his gaze was on the forest.

"Men." She let out a huff. "Sometimes a

man's misguided attempt to help only makes things worse."

"How do you figure I made things worse?" He tucked in his chin and stared her down.

A guilty flush for having ventured into the woods alone had her biting her tongue.

"Call for backup," he instructed before he returned to his scrutiny of the woods.

Fighting back the urge to snap at him for issuing her orders, she used the radio attached to her uniform belt.

"Willow, everything okay?" Jackson's voice came at her, eliciting a sense of déjà vu. For a moment, her pulse spiked as she recalled the last time she'd called him and he'd asked that question. The trail marker had exploded. Giving herself a mental shake, she quickly explained the situation. "I'm turning on my GPS beacon. I need a crime scene unit here."

"Tell me you're okay," Jackson insisted.

"I'm with Theo. We're okay."

"Where are Brandie and Parker?"

"Still at the Stark Lodge." Later she'd have to deal with the fallout of having left her shadows—Theo and the two candidates—behind.

She clicked off with Jackson and turned on her beacon. "They'll be here soon."

Theo eased away from her to inspect the felled cedar. Willow and Star hurried along with him. Star's nose moved along the tree's massive trunk until she sat at the exposed and charred remains of the stump, where explosives had been used on the backside of the tree.

Her phone dinged with an incoming text. Figuring it was Jackson, she fished her phone from her pocket. She didn't recognize the number. She opened the text message. Five words on the screen screamed at her.

Stay out of my way.

SEVEN

"Willow?" Concern arced through Theo. Willow's face drained of color, and she looked like she might be sick. Whatever she'd read on the text message had upset her. Or was it a delayed reaction to almost being crushed by the felled tree? Or the kiss after?

She'd surprised and humbled him. All the feelings he'd been suppressing for so long rose to the surface, making his heart ache with longing. When she'd broken away from him, it had taken all his willpower not to pull her close again and tell her... Tell her what? That he loved her still? That he didn't want to lose her? He couldn't.

Giving himself a mental head slap, he was at her side in two strides. Theo took Willow's trembling hands in his and gently pried the phone from her fingers. Her grip tightened for a second, and then she let go.

Theo read the text.

Stay out of my way.

A spike of fear pumped through his veins, followed closely by anger.

If this wasn't proof that somebody had just tried to hurt Willow and their child, he didn't know what was. Determination solidified in his veins. He was going to get the creep who was threatening his family.

If he hadn't been here to save Willow, she would've been crushed.

Someone was watching her.

Someone had her phone number.

He would do everything in his power to end this. First thing, he would tap into the FBI resources. His buddy Jimmy Freeland was the best technological whiz Theo had ever met.

Willow visibly pulled herself together. "I need to send the phone number to Jasmin, our tech expert, at headquarters."

"I want my guy to take a crack at it first."

Willow frowned. "Jasmin is good. We do just fine here at the PNK9 Unit."

"I'm not saying she isn't skilled at her job, but my guy's the best."

Theo held her gaze, unwilling to back down. Finally, she gave a sharp nod and turned to Star. "Search." She allowed Star to lead her away.

Theo's pulse raced. What if there was another explosive device in the area? Star would find it, putting them all in danger again.

"Stay put," he told her, barely resisting the urge to snatch her back to his side.

Willow paused and glanced over her shoulder. Her eyes cracked with fire. "You're not my boss. And soon you won't even be my husband. You have no say in what I do."

So much for the woman who'd kissed him just for being alive. And he could play hardball, too. "But I do. You're carrying my child. That gives me the right to—"

Willow marched up to him, getting in his face. Star followed obediently, then sat and stared up at them as if watching a tennis match. "You have the right?" She jabbed her finger into his chest. "I have the right to know *why*. Why did you push me away and destroy our marriage?"

Theo swallowed back the bile rising into his throat. He hadn't expected her to go *there*. Not now, after all this time. "Willow." He didn't know what to say. Shame and guilt vied for dominance. It was easier to concentrate on the case rather than their relationship. "Somehow the bomber got your number."

"It's not like it's a state secret," she said. "I hand my card out all the time."

"So I noticed."

"Obviously, the bomber has been watching me," Willow said. "He—"

"Or she."

Willow inclined her head in acknowledgment. "Or she texted, 'Stay out of my way.' I take it that means he *or she* has more explosions planned. This area is the entrance to the all-terrain vehicle trail. The bomber obviously is sabotaging the route."

"That would be my guess." Theo couldn't keep the hard edge out of his voice. "I'd really like to ask Donovan to assign someone else to this park for the time being. You need to get out of harm's way."

"We've gone through this already, Theo. Just because I'm pregnant doesn't mean I can't work. There are plenty of law enforcement officers who stay on the job until they're at least six months along."

"Now that we know the bomber is targeting you," Theo said, "it changes things."

"Not really. We're being careful. I'm being careful—"

"Except for coming out here by yourself—"

"I left a *note*. Which you saw. And now you're here providing backup. The only way I'll be truly safe is to work the case and discover who's behind the attacks." She gave an exasperated huff and turned away from him again. "Do what you're going to do. *We're* going to see if we can find any evidence that might help identify this bomber."

Theo closed his eyes as deep pain spread through his chest. He pushed it away and focused on what he needed to do—Theo sent Jimmy the phone number the threatening text came from, then called him.

"Hey, dude," Jimmy said upon answering. "Heard you were back home in Washington State. Things working out better?"

Theo grimaced. Jimmy was the only one he'd confided in that his marriage was over.

Keeping an eye on Willow and Star as they worked the scene, Theo said, "A lot has happened. I sent you a number. I need you to find out everything you can about the sender."

"Sure. What's happening?"

"Someone from that number planted explosives in the state park and… Willow's pregnant."

"Dude, don't bury the lead! You're going to be a daddy!"

"Yes. But we're separated, remember? She filed for divorce. And someone's trying to hurt her."

Jimmy gave a whistle. "What are you going to do?"

Theo stared at the text on Willow's phone.

"I have to protect her and catch the sicko terrorizing the parks and threatening her."

"Okay," Jimmy said, "that's a good plan. But what about the future? You have to talk to her, man. Tell her what happened."

Theo shook his head. "No. Never. I can't."

Jimmy's sigh was heavy through the line. "Dude, that's messed up. I can't see this ending well unless you do. Xavier's death is not on you."

Nausea rolled through Theo's gut. "Yes, it is. Look, can you work your skills and locate the person who sent the text or not?"

"I'll do my best," Jimmy said, his voice firm. "That's all any of us can ever do."

"I owe you, bud."

"Talk to your wife." Jimmy clicked off.

Theo rubbed a hand over his jaw. He did need to talk to Willow and tell her what happened. But how did he find the words? Opening up and admitting he'd failed would be the hardest thing he'd ever done. Willow's disappointment would crush him.

Willow's heart still pumped too hard and too fast in her chest. Theo was the most aggravating man she'd ever met.

One minute he was saving her life and the next trying to tell her what to do.

And in between, she'd kissed him.

She could only claim a moment of adrenaline-laced-with-fear-induced lapse in judgment.

Star, her nose to the ground, led Willow away from the toppled tree. Obviously, her partner had caught the scent of something. The bomber? Where would the scent trail lead?

Willow glanced over her shoulder, her gaze meeting Theo's. He raised an eyebrow. Her rebellious nature wanted to continue off into the woods alone. But she knew having done that once and almost being crushed had been a mistake. If Theo hadn't been here... She didn't know if she and Star could have made it far enough away from the tree in time. But Theo's quick thinking, and his athletic ability—to not only pick her up but run with her—was a feat that had to have been born out of adrenaline and fear. Fear for her safety.

Her heart cramped. For whatever reason, he was willing to let their marriage die, but he wasn't willing to let *her* die. That had to count for something, right?

His actions meant he was a decent human being. Not that he still loved her or cared about her in any special way. He'd already made it clear he didn't want to stay married to her. Or he would've fought her when she said she was filing for divorce. But he hadn't. He'd accepted her suggestion of ending their marriage the same way he used to accept her suggestion of pasta rather than chicken for dinner.

Star sat and stared at the ground. Willow stepped close, wariness tightening the muscles along her neck and shoulders. Filtered sunlight coming through the canopy of trees overhead glinted off something metal wedged in the dirt. Reeling Star back a couple paces and telling her to stay, Willow squatted down to investigate the protruding item. Her pulse spiked as recognition blossomed. A blasting cap. The small metal container used to set off explosives housed a tiny charge which could still be dangerous.

Theo had her phone, and she needed to photograph the evidence. "Theo," she called out. "Here."

Theo jogged over and squatted beside her. "Is that...?"

"A blasting cap." She held out her hand. "Phone."

He handed her phone over. She photographed the protruding object. From her utility belt she took out a collapsible place marker and wrote the time and date, before placing it over the blasting cap.

"Once the crime scene techs safely remove

this, it will go to Bartholomew," she said. "Hopefully he can get fingerprints or DNA or some trace element of evidence that will help us find this person."

"That's a good find."

She rose and so did Theo.

"My buddy Jimmy is going to see if he can locate where that text originated."

Willow didn't want to resent his help. But she did. "I'm going to send the text to Jasmin and see if she can do it. Between the two of them—"

"—we should be able to find the texter." Theo finished her sentence.

A wave of sadness washed over Willow. There used to be a time when they would smile at each other when that happened. And then usually kiss.

She couldn't let a kiss happen again, no matter how right it felt or how much she missed him. She turned away to send the threatening texter's number to Jasmin at the PNK9 headquarters.

"Willow." Theo's voice sounded raw.

Her gaze whipped to him, and the pain in his expression made her want to reach out to him.

"I need to tell you something."

Pulse pounding, Willow braced herself. Was he finally going to spill why he no longer loved her?

"I—"

Star let out a series of barks, cutting off his words. The sound of people moving through the woods surrounded them. Willow and Theo both reached for their weapons while turning so that they were back to back, prepared to face whatever threat was coming their way.

Willow relaxed as her fellow PNK9 Unit members, Jackson Dean with his partner, a Doberman pinscher named Rex, and Asher Gilmore with his partner, an English springer spaniel named Spark, along with the four candidates and their dogs, materialized out of the woods and entered the clearing.

"You were saying?" Willow prompted, turning back to Theo.

He shook his head. His expression hardened to granite. "Later."

Whatever he'd been about to confess to her would have to wait. When he finally opened up, what would he tell her? And why was she so afraid to hear what he had to say?

Concern bracketed Jackson's eyes as he moved to where they stood. "You two okay?"

"Yes." Willow explained about the tree and the evidence Star had found.

"What were you doing out here?" Asher asked, joining them. The candidates had fanned out, providing a barrier.

"Searching for clues," Theo answered before Willow could. She slanted him a glance, at once grateful he hadn't revealed her jaunt out into the woods alone but at the same time miffed that he thought he needed to shield her. And even more miffed his protection made her heart melt a little.

"There are plans to put an all-terrain vehicle trail through the middle of the forest," Theo continued. "Starting here." He gestured toward the clearing. "With a parking lot scheduled there." He pointed to the wooded area toward the highway.

Jackson frowned, his gaze scanning the area. "That explains the heavy-duty equipment we saw."

"We think the bomber may be an ecoterrorist trying to stop the trail," Theo said.

"A good theory. Provable?" Asher asked.

"My boss contacted the group lobbying for the trail," Theo said. "They've had threats, mostly letters, and someone graffitied the outside of their headquarters in Seattle."

"When did you learn this?" Willow asked.

Theo turned his censuring gaze on her. "Before we came out here. I was planning to tell you, but you had left."

Oh. Willow mentally winced. He'd come looking for her to tell her this news. "Suspects?"

"Not so far," Theo said.

Not surprised but disappointed there were no leads on that front, Willow turned to Asher. "Any news on Mara?"

Asher and Mara were half siblings who shared the same father, but they hadn't grown up together and weren't close, even as colleagues. Still, Willow hoped Asher would be up on the latest information regarding Mara.

"She called me and I talked with her, briefly. She says she's innocent. But she wouldn't tell me where she was or where she was going. I let the chief know she got in touch, but there was no way to trace the call."

Willow's chest ached over missing her friend's attempt to reach out to her. "You believe her, right?"

Asher's jaw firmed. "It doesn't look good for her."

Irritation flushed through Willow. "That's not an answer."

"I have to stay objective," Asher said, his grim tone grating on Willow. "I'll be taken off this case if I'm not. She and I hardly know each other. Yes, we'd started to build a relationship the six months prior to—" He ran a hand through his short blond hair. "Just because we share the same father…" He grimaced. "We have to follow the evidence."

Willow could tell he was torn up about his half sister and trying hard not to show it. Her ire waned. "I'm going to continue to pray that the evidence proves she is innocent. I know in my gut she didn't do what she's accused of."

"I don't know what to tell you, Willow." He took out his phone. "I'm going to call for the crime scene techs to sweep the area. I'll stick around with the candidates."

She pointed out the blasting cap she'd found to Asher, knowing he'd keep it secure until it could be safely removed. The unit was stretched thin between the various issues going on in the parks. First with the murders of Stacey Stark and Jonas Digby. Then the attempted kidnapping of Stacey Stark's brother's child.

Willow was thankful that Mara hadn't been implicated in the attempted kidnapping. Or in the danger that had brought fellow team member Colt Maxwell and Mount Rainier park ranger Brooke Stevens together. The identical twin sister whom Brooke hadn't known about had been killing hikers—and framing Brooke. In the final showdown, the malicious twin had injured Willow, and Brooke had sat with Willow in the hospital after she learned of the pregnancy.

Willow put her hand on her abdomen. Should she feel a flutter soon?

Theo stepped up, putting his hand at her elbow. "Are you okay?"

Annoyed by the situation, she snapped, "I'm so sick of that question."

He gave her a crooked grin that did funny things to her insides. "You have to admit, it's the subject on everybody's mind."

She heaved a sigh. It was hard to fault the concern of others when she was clearly a target now. She'd be upset if one of her friends and colleagues had come close to being hurt, as she had.

Willow's cell rang. It was Jasmin.

"Sorry to say," Jasmin said, "the text came from a burner phone. Untraceable. Though I did manage to figure out that the burner phone was somewhere within the Olympic National Forest. But I couldn't pinpoint the location. It pinged off a tower at the top of Hurricane Ridge. It could be within a hundred-mile radius."

"Thank you," Willow said. She hung up.

"Hopefully, Jimmy will get something more," Theo said. "Let's get back to the lodge. There's nothing more we can do here."

Leaving the scene in the hands of her team members, Willow, Star and Theo headed back to the Stark Lodge. The two candidates, Brandie and Parker, followed behind.

When they reached the lodge, they headed for the elevators. Through the big picture window in the lobby overlooking the parking lot, Willow caught sight of fellow PNK9 Unit officer Ruby Orton getting out of a large pickup truck. The man driving the truck climbed out and met her at the tailgate.

Surprise washed over Willow. She recognized Eli Ballard from the photos the chief had shown the unit. Tall, muscular beneath his suit, with short dark hair and bright blue eyes. What was Ruby doing with Eli?

They stood very close together, and a sweet look passed between them before Ruby gave Eli a hug. Then she moved past him and headed for her own personal vehicle. Willow hadn't noticed Ruby's car earlier, but then, she hadn't been looking for it. Were the two dating?

Willow snagged Theo's arm. "Eli Ballard is back."

They watched Eli walk toward the employee entrance.

But a stocky man with a mop of dark curly hair stopped Eli before he could enter the lodge. They seemed to be having an argument.

"Who's that with him?" Theo asked.

"Maybe an employee?" she guessed. "A disgruntled one by the looks of it."

The two men parted ways, with Eli going

inside and the stocky man hurrying off to the parking lot.

"Let's go have a chat with Mr. Ballard," Theo said.

At the reception desk, the same young woman from the day before, Janet, smiled at them. "Can I help you with anything?"

"We saw Eli Ballard return."

Janet's eyes widened, and she picked up the phone. "I'll let him know you're here."

Willow reached across the desk and put her finger on the disconnect button. "I'd rather you didn't." She and Theo walked over to the swinging door.

Janet bit her lip, indecision clear on her face.

Willow prompted, "This is a police matter."

Janet nodded. Theo led the way down the hall. They halted at the closed door of Eli's office. Willow knocked and then stepped inside without waiting for a reply. Both she and Theo held up their badges.

Eli Ballard sat behind his desk. He glanced up, irritation flashing in his cornflower-blue eyes before his expression cleared and he pasted on a smile. He stood. "Officer Bates?"

"Mr. Ballard."

Eli's gaze bounced from Willow to Star to Theo. His eyebrows rose. "The FBI is involved in this? I didn't know Stacey's death would garner quite this much attention. But I'm glad." He gestured for them to sit across from him in leather armchairs. Willow sat and gestured for Star to lie down beside her.

"You're glad?" Theo asked.

"Of course," Eli said emphatically. "My business partner was killed. We've all been grieving. It's been almost three months with no answers."

"Were you close to Stacey Stark?" Willow asked.

Eli's gaze snapped to her. "We were close. Like family. Hard to be partners with somebody for as long as we were without that kind of relationship developing. But I've told all this to several different police officers."

"We're more interested in what you have behind the basement door," Theo said.

For a moment, Eli stared at them blankly, then his expression bloomed with surprise. Real? Or a mask to throw them off?

EIGHT

"The basement?" Eli sputtered. "Why are you interested in—"

"My partner is a bomb and weapons detection dog," Willow said, gauging his reaction. "She alerted at that door."

Eli eyed Star. "Of course, she did. What a good dog." To Willow and Theo, he said, "The door is locked because we've had trouble with previous employees swiping things from the lodge and restaurant. I have some very valuable collector items down in the basement."

"Collector items?" Theo questioned.

"Unfortunately, I had to take my eighty-five-year-old grandfather's weapons away from him. He's getting a little senile, you know. He and my father were avid hunters." Eli shrugged, making a face. "I like hunting for the most part. But I'm not rabid about the sport like my dad and grandpa."

"You won't mind showing us?" Theo asked.

Eli's chin tucked in. "Of course not. Are you a hunter, too?"

"Of a sort," Theo said.

Willow stomach twisted. She knew Theo didn't mean hunting animals or wildlife. Theo was a hunter of the human sort.

Eli opened a drawer in his desk and pulled out a ring of keys. "Follow me. I take any opportunity I get to show off this collection."

He led them to the basement door and quickly unlocked it. Star gave her passive alert again, which only confirmed to Willow that there were indeed weapons below.

Eli started to go first, but Theo put a hand up to stop him. "I'll go first."

Eli shrugged good-naturedly. "You're the boss."

"Really, you're the boss now that Stacey Stark is gone, correct?" Willow asked as she descended the stairs behind Theo.

When they reached the bottom landing, Eli said, "Yes, I am. I have a couple of managers who rotate between the properties. We always try to have at least one person in management at each lodge, but with Stacey..." Eli sighed. "It's been difficult without her."

Willow noticed there were no visible weapons in the storage area.

Eli led the way to a large cabinet, which he unlocked and opened, revealing at least eight different types of hunting rifles. Some looked very old but well cared for. Boxes of ammo sat on the floor of the cabinet. Eli had been telling the truth.

Willow exchanged a glance with Theo. He took a quick picture of the inventory. Then indicated for Eli to close the cabinet back up.

"Have there been any new developments in Stacey's murder?" Eli asked as he headed up the stairs.

"The PNK9 team is investigating around the clock," Willow told him. "I'm sure we will discover something soon to identify the killer."

Eli locked the basement door once they were through and turned to stare at her. "I thought the killer was already identified—Mara Gilmore, Jonas Digby's old girlfriend."

Willow's heart sank. She hated that even civilians thought Mara was guilty. Though she should be innocent until proven guilty, Willow knew in the court of public opinion that's not how it worked. Mara was guilty until she was proven innocent. The media made sure to taint any potential jurors with their theories and innuendos. Regardless of the fact there was no hard evidence.

Willow had to do her job and make sure that justice was served. She knew her teammates would follow the letter of the law in bringing Mara in for questioning as well as determining who actually did kill Stacey Stark and Jonas Digby. But of course, she couldn't say any of that to Eli Ballard. She could barely say it to Theo and not have him give her a lecture on being unable to know what was going on in another person's heart.

Just as she had no idea what was going on inside Theo's heart. And the lack of knowledge was more painful with every moment they spent together. It was time they talked, and she wasn't going to let him squirm out of it.

Once they were back in the presidential suite, she said, "You started to tell me something earlier. What was it?"

Theo's heart pounded in his chest. An anxious ball of nerves ricocheted through his gut. This was it. The moment he'd been dreading for a year. Guilt swamped him. Self-loathing was quick on its heels, making his pulse throb at his temples. All the horror of that day came rushing back as he moved to stand in front of the floor-to-ceiling sliding glass doors overlooking the back of the Stark Lodge.

Behind him he heard Willow moving, then heard the creak of the leather couch as she took a seat.

"Theo, you know you can tell me anything."

Was that true? There had been a time when he never questioned telling her everything that was going on with him. But now... He turned to face her.

Star sat next to her on the sofa. Willow had tucked her feet off to the side, having taken off her shoes. Her light brown hair had been released from her ponytail and cascaded over her shoulders. So beautiful. This woman was going to bear his child. This woman, whom he had once loved with every fiber of his being, until guilt, shame and self-hatred had choked that love out. He ran a hand through his hair. He realized he was stalling.

Just get it over with, his conscience screamed.

Once he opened Pandora's box, there would be no way to go back. Telling Willow the truth would make it clear to her that he was undeserving of her love. And it would kill what little remained between them.

Bracing himself for the inevitable, he said, "Eighteen months ago, I went undercover in a chop shop run by a crew of car thieves who were targeting various areas of Florida, stripping the cars and selling the parts. But we suspected there was more to it. I befriended a young mechanic who vouched for me and brought me on with the crew."

The words spilled out, faster and faster. "Xavier was only twenty years old. He worked in the chop shops to provide for his mom and sisters, but he knew what they were doing in the shop was illegal. And he'd stumbled across more than just auto parts being stripped from vehicles. It seemed this particular crew was being used to move illegal weapons."

Theo took a seat in the leather chair and braced his elbows on his knees. He couldn't meet Willow's gaze. "Six months into the undercover assignment, things went south."

Theo rubbed his forehead. The horror replaying over in his mind was on a never-ending loop. "Even though they let me work in the shops, I could never get close enough to the boss. But Xavier could. I sent Xavier into the inner sanctum with a hidden camera. I promised him I would protect him. I promised him I would protect his family."

"What happened?"

Willow's soft question stabbed into him like a dagger.

"They discovered the camera. They killed Xavier and videoed his death, then sent the video back to the FBI."

Willow made a distressed sound, and still Theo couldn't look at her.

"I shouldn't have sent him in there. I should never have recruited him. I should've found another way to insert myself into this illegal crew. I should've been better prepared to intervene. But I was too selfish. I didn't want to blow my cover. I wanted to win more than I wanted to take precautions." His insides twisting, his voice came out on a tremble. "It's my fault, and I can't make it right."

He heard Willow moving, and then she was there, kneeling before him and taking his hands in hers.

"We both know the risks involved in what we do. You know you aren't responsible for this young man's death. The person who killed him is."

Theo shook his head as a protest rose. "No. It's my fault." He tried to retract his hands, but she wouldn't let go. "I failed. I walked out of there and he didn't."

"What happened to his mother and sisters?"

"We relocated them. I owed Xavier."

She cupped his face. "You have survivor's guilt. You need to talk to a professional."

Theo barked out a harsh laugh and rose, forcing her to let go of him. He moved away from her. "I did talk to someone. An FBI psychologist."

"And they let you go back out to the field, knowing you're suffering?" Anger laced her words.

His lips twisted in a wry grimace. "I knew what to say. Remember, I deceive people for a living. It wasn't hard to convince the psychologist I was putting the blame where it should go."

"But why would you fake that? Why won't you get the help you need? It's obviously eating you up inside. And it's destroyed our marriage." She stood next to him, her hand warm on his forearm. "Seek counseling with me. We have a child to think about."

His heart bled at the mention of bringing a child into the world. Into this mess, where danger lurked around every corner. "Counseling won't change the past. Nothing will bring Xavier back. I've worked hard this past year to bring down Raman Nugent, the man who pulled the trigger. Even putting him behind bars hasn't released me from the responsibility or the shame and guilt."

"Please, Theo. Agree to go to counseling with me."

"No. I don't deserve it. I don't deserve you."

She fisted her hands on her hips. "So you

would rather destroy your life, our life together, as some sort of penitence for something you had no control over?"

"But I did have control. I could've refused to send him in. I could've stopped it."

"And possibly gotten yourself killed in the process." She shook her head, anger sparking from her eyes. "You're punishing yourself. But you're punishing me, as well. And our baby." She stepped back, putting distance between them. "You're hiding behind this giant wall you've built up, and I can't scale it. You won't let down the bridge."

Theo's knees weakened as the truth of her words slammed into him. He dropped his head against the cool glass of the floor-to-ceiling window.

"I don't know how this is going to work between us." Her voice broke on such deep sorrow it sent more pain ricocheting through him. "I don't know if I can have you near our child like this."

He flinched. His world crumbled around him. The proverbial wall caved in on him. How did he pick up the pieces?

The ringing of Willow's cell phone shuddered through him. He snapped to attention, pushing away from the glass, and sought her gaze. Another warning from the bomber? *Please, no.*

He held his breath as she hurried across the room and scooped up her phone.

"It's Donovan." She clutched the phone to her chest.

Theo breathed in with relief. She disappeared into her bedroom.

Star leaned against Theo's leg as if offering her support. He sank to his knees and hugged the dog, wishing it was as easy to accept support from Willow.

"Donovan? Is everything okay?" Willow asked as she tried to focus on her boss and not on all that Theo had confessed. Her heart ached with sorrow and anger. The senselessness of a young man's death and the undeserved guilt and shame Theo had taken ownership of, ruining their lives.

"I should be asking you that question." Donovan's voice boomed in her ear, reminding her of how close they'd come to death today. "I heard about you almost getting crushed by a tree."

She grimaced with the memory of the tree crashing through the woods and slamming against the ground. She shuddered. "We found a blasting cap in the area. Hopefully, Bartholomew can pull a fingerprint or DNA."

Donovan grunted. "How are the candidates working out? What are your impressions of them?"

Raising her eyebrows at the change in topic, she considered his questions. "I think they're both competent. Eager. Parker is a bit of a braggart, but he handles his dog well. They seem well bonded."

She thought about Brandie and her comments about people being forced to do something against their will. Not knowing if it was just talk or something the younger woman had experienced herself, Willow decided not to mention that conversation. "Brandie is very accomplished. She handles Taz well, but the dog is a bit spun up. She could use some more focused attention and training. Though I don't know what discipline she has decided on."

"We're still working out the kinks, trying to cover any holes we might have in the unit. Keep an eye on those two. I'm going to have you keep them with you a little longer. Utilize them as best you can and as you see fit. They will learn a lot from you. You're one of my best officers."

Her mouth quirked, because she knew he said that to each of them. "Thanks, Donovan. I do appreciate the extra sets of eyes. We think we might have the motivation as to why the bomber is targeting the park." She told the chief about the all-terrain vehicle trail. "Someone may be trying to sabotage the potential route."

"The warning you received is worrisome," Donovan stated. "I want you to use extreme caution as you proceed."

Putting her hand on her abdomen, she nodded. "Don't worry. I'm being careful. And Theo's here making sure that nothing will happen." But soon he would go back to DC. And if he didn't get help... She gave herself a shake and turned her attention to other matters. "Brandie has an interesting theory about Mara. She thinks maybe Mara's not coming in because she's afraid of something. Something beyond being suspected of murdering Stacey Stark and Jonas Digby."

"That thought has been bounced around. But until we find Mara, we won't know what's going on. Jasmin told me about the phone call that you received from Mara. If you receive any more contact, call me directly."

"I will, sir. Thank you."

Willow hung up and stared out the window at the trees beyond the lodge property. The sky was a pretty blue with the sun high in the sky. *Where are you, Mara?*

Willow could really use a friend to unpack

the revelation of why Theo had been pushing her away for the past year.

The ding of an incoming text zipped along Willow's frayed nerves.

A number she didn't recognize popped up. Her pulse sped up. Mara?

Or another text from the bomber?

Anticipation revved along her flesh. She swiped and loaded the text message. Her heart caught in her throat. The words leaped out at her.

It's a bad day to be at the kiddie pool.

Kiddie pool?

Dread and horror spread through Willow. Would the bomber really hurt children?

Theo sat at the dining room table. After Willow had retreated to her room to talk to her boss, he'd forced himself to concentrate on something other than the past. He spread out the Mara Gilmore case files that Donovan had sent over for his perusal. Everything seemed to be stacked against Mara. Almost too well. As a forensic investigator, Mara Gilmore was either very incompetent or she was being framed. If Willow was to be believed, Mara was a good person, and she had to be smart if she'd been hired on with the K-9 unit.

But who would want to frame her for murder? And why?

Willow burst from her bedroom. Theo's heart jumped into his throat. Immediately, his thoughts went to the baby. Was something wrong? Holding his breath, he stood as Willow skidded to a halt in front of him.

Without a word, she thrust her phone at him.

He forced his gaze from her panic-stricken face to read the words on the screen, his stomach dropping. It's a bad day to be at the kiddie pool. "Where is there a kiddie pool in the park?"

"There are many swimming holes in the various lakes and waterfalls, but the only one that I know that is designated for children is at the hot springs resort. We've got to go. I'll call it in on the way."

Willow didn't waste any time leashing up Star. Theo wanted to demand she stay behind. But he knew she would only balk. It was up to him to keep her safe. He grabbed the keys to the SUV. "You better alert Jackson and the candidates."

He would do his best to keep Willow as far from the radius of any explosion as he could.

Willow took her phone back and quickly

called Jackson, filling him in as she pulled on her shoes. She hung up and headed for the door. "Jackson and the others will meet us there."

Theo drove as fast as he dared on the winding road leading to the posh hot springs resort in the middle of the Olympic National Forest. The sprawling resort with its peaked roofs and stone masonry sat smack-dab in the middle of an oasis of old-growth trees and tapped into natural hot spring water.

He'd barely parked before Willow hopped out. She and Star headed for the pools. "Wait!"

"No time," she called over her shoulder. "You better let the hotel know."

Parker and Brandie pulled up alongside Theo.

"Evacuate the premises. Gather everyone on the far side of the parking lot," Theo instructed, then he took off at a run for the resort manager's office.

Inside the beautifully appointed hotel with its gleaming hardwood floors, crystal chandeliers and colorful rugs, he approached the front desk, flashed his FBI badge and asked to see the site manager. A few moments later, a tall, middle-aged woman with graying hair pulled back into a severe bun joined him. "What can I do for you?"

"Theo Bates, FBI. We've had a bomb threat."

Her eyes went wide, her mouth opened. "Here?"

"Yes. I need you to evacuate. My partner and her bomb-sniffing dog are at the pool area. The threat was specifically for the kiddie pool."

"Oh, my." She placed a hand at the base of her throat. "Should we pull the fire alarm?"

"Yes, do that."

The woman nodded and hurried off. A few moments later, the fire alarm shrieked through the air. Theo hustled outside to the pools, where Willow followed behind Star. The dog ran her snout along every chair, every backpack, every towel and every crevice surrounding the pools. People milled about, watching the pair.

"Everybody out. Don't worry about your stuff," Theo shouted, urging people to move.

A preschooler ran into the wading pool. A woman, holding an infant, stood at the edge, urging him to come out.

"Get that kid out of the pool!" Theo stormed toward them.

The mother waded in. "Lawrence, come out this instant. You are in so much trouble." The kid evaded his mother's grasp, splashing water and giggling.

Theo glanced over to see where Willow was. She and Star were working their way around one of the larger pools. He'd hazard a guess she'd already checked the wading pool, but to be safe he needed to get the kid and his mother far from the area.

He charged into the pool, scooped up the kid from behind and carried him out of the pool. The little boy screamed, the sound rivaling the fire alarm.

The mother hurried to catch up. "Thank you."

Theo set the squirming kid on his feet but kept a firm grip on his shoulder. "Stay with your mother."

Lawrence blinked up at him and grasped his mother's outstretched hand. The pair hurried off with the other guests. He watched them with a hitch in his chest. And it hit him forcefully—he was going to be a father. There was no way for him to compartmentalize Willow's pregnancy. If he wanted to be a part of his child's life, he was going to have to make some changes.

Shoes sloshing water with every step, Theo stalked over to where Willow and Star were clearing the towel hut. "Anything?"

"Nothing. I started with the wading pool, thinking maybe there was something hidden in the filter. But nothing was there. Nothing here at all."

This was a hoax? Some sick game the bomber was playing to mess with Willow? To what end? "That's it. You are off this case."

Theo's decree reverberated against Willow's eardrums as her mind scrambled to make sense of the words. They'd had this conversation. She wasn't going to have it again.

Instead of acknowledging him, she turned away and surveyed the area. For whatever reason, the bomber was toying with her. Frustration beat a steady rhythm against her eyes. She needed water. And to calm down.

Theo reached for her hand, his fingers threading through hers.

"Listen to me," he said, drawing her gaze. "This could have ended very badly. Not just for you, but for all these people. And our child. The bomber is unpredictable. This was a false alarm, but next time it might not be. Obviously, he doesn't care who he puts in harm's way. As long as he is fixated on you, people could be hurt. Do you want that on your conscience?"

Empathy squeezed her heart. Now that she understood he blamed himself for something he couldn't have controlled, compassion filled her veins. Warding off the rebellious anger rising up, she heaved a sigh and collected herself. "We need to search the whole premises. The pool could've been a misdirect."

She held up her hand when he opened his mouth to protest. "But to be on the safe side, when the bomb squad gets here, I will put on protective gear before checking out the rest of the hotel. Satisfied?"

For a long moment, he stared at her. She lifted her chin, letting him know she wouldn't back down. Finally, he gave a sharp nod. "That'll have to do."

The Washington State Patrol's bomb technicians arrived. Willow put on the protective covering provided by the technicians, which allowed her and Star, accompanied by two other similarly geared troopers, to search the hotel.

Three hours later, having found no explosive devices, Willow and Theo rode in silence back to the Stark Lodge. Willow mulled over the purpose of sending her and Star on a fruitless hunt.

At the hotel, she headed to her room and let Star off her leash. Needing to freshen up, Willow went into the bathroom and rinsed her face with cold water. Star barked, the sound familiar and dreadful. She was alerting on something.

Willow hurried from the bathroom to find Star sitting at the balcony door. A prickling sensation at the nape of Willow's neck had her quickly grabbing the leash and calling Star to her side. After hooking the leash to Star's collar, Willow yanked open the bedroom door and charged out into the living room.

"Theo!"

Within seconds, Theo's bedroom door opened and he strode out, barefoot in lounge pants and a T-shirt.

Her breath caught at the sight of him, but she couldn't allow herself to be distracted. "Star alerted at my balcony door."

Without hesitation, Theo crossed the room to grip her elbow and tugged her out the suite door. "We need to evacuate. Clearly, the threat at the kiddie pool was a misdirect, after all."

Theo pulled the fire alarm and then started banging on doors. Willow followed suit. Within fifteen minutes, they had the Stark Lodge evacuated. When Willow wanted to go and search the rest of the lodge, Theo held her at bay. "Just like at the resort, you have to wait until the bomb squad gets here. I'm not going to lose you."

NINE

Standing outside the lodge with the evacuated guests, Theo fought the helplessness cascading through his veins. The bomb squad had arrived and geared up to go inside, Willow included. He hated being sidelined while Willow did her job. All he could do was watch her, once again dressed from head to toe in protective gear, and Star, wearing her ballistic-proof vest with the PNK9 Unit logo, disappear inside the lodge with the other Washington State Patrol bomb technicians who'd arrived on the scene.

Every moment that ticked by ratcheted up his anxiety. Had the bomber set more explosives in the lodge? How had the unidentified suspect gained access to Willow's balcony? Was the person a lodge employee?

Finally, Willow, Star and the bomb technicians emerged from the lodge, and relief washed over Theo, nearly bringing him to his knees. He hurried forward, wincing as bits of gravel and dirt bit into his bare feet. A reminder of how shaken he'd been by Star's alert.

Willow removed her helmet. She looked shaken, too. "No other bombs. Just the one at my sliding glass door."

One of the bomb technicians stepped up. He was an older man with graying hair and a thick mustache. "It was a good thing she didn't open that slider. The second the door ran on the tracks, it would've exploded, taking out that whole side of the hotel."

Theo's heart thudded with dread. He needed to get Willow away from here, away from the bomber. He could take her to DC, far from the bomber's reach. As soon as she was out of her protective gear, he snagged her elbow and directed her and Star to where Jackson and the recruits stood.

"Willow and I are leaving," he announced.

Willow jerked her elbow from his grasp. "No, we're not. I am not giving the bomber that much power over me or the situation."

"Your presence here puts everyone in danger," Theo argued.

"He's played his hand," Willow returned. "He wouldn't dare try something here again. He'll have to realize we'll be on guard and waiting for him to make a move."

Theo growled in his throat. He didn't like it, but what she said was logical. Still, he'd feel better removing her from the line of fire and hiding her away. Forever if need be. But running wouldn't fly. Willow would balk.

"We need to look at the security footage of the property," Jackson interjected. "See if we can identify him and how he was able to rig a bomb on your balcony."

Theo stared at Jackson. "You don't agree Willow should leave?"

"Not my call," Jackson said. "That's something you need to talk to Donovan about. Though you won't hold much sway, considering you're here as a courtesy and are too emotionally involved, Special Agent Bates."

The use of his title sent a flush of aggravation through Theo. He could throw the bureau's weight around if he chose, but he wouldn't. Doing so wouldn't garner him much goodwill with the team or Willow. He held her gaze. "Fine. We stay, but we are not going back to those rooms."

"I can live with that," Willow said. "Let's pack up."

Back inside the hotel, while Jackson and the candidates went to talk to hotel security, Theo secured adjoining rooms on the second floor overlooking the parking lot. He, Willow and

Star made quick work of transferring their belongings from the presidential suite to the new set of accommodations. Nice rooms, but not as spacious.

Theo changed into fresh clothes and knocked on the interior door to Willow's room.

"Come in."

He pushed the door open. Willow, wearing yoga pants and a long-sleeve shirt, sat on the middle of the bed, eating a bag of banana chips. Star lay curled next to her. Tenderness flooded him. His two hearts. And one day there'd be a third added. He'd been a fool to think he could ever live without Willow, Star and, soon, his child in his life.

Willow offered up the bag. "Snack?"

There was so much he had to make up for. So much damage to repair, he wasn't even sure how or where to begin. He knew what she wanted but couldn't do it. Leaning against the doorjamb, he shook his head. "No. Thanks. Willow, promise me you won't leave without telling me."

She gave him a wry smile. "I promise. No more traipsing off without you."

Her words speared through him. He'd broken the promises he'd made to her when they married. Love and honor, cherish and protect. In sickness and in health. Vows he'd made before their friends. Before God. And he'd stomped on them. On his love for Willow. And her love for him. Because he couldn't face his failure that had cost the life of another.

Could she forgive him? He wanted to ask, but the words wouldn't form. Better to stay on task. The danger to Willow had to be dealt with before he could contemplate how to move forward. "Let's go see what Jackson discovered from security."

She scrambled to her feet. "Give me five minutes."

He backed out of the room, shutting the door behind him. Exactly five minutes later, she knocked. He opened the door to discover she'd changed into her uniform, braided her hair and had Star on leash. He always marveled at how quickly she could be ready to roll.

They found Jackson and his Doberman, Rex, in the lobby. Rex and Star greeted each other and settled on the cool hardwood floor side by side.

"Where are the candidates?" Willow asked.

"Owen and Veronica are on their way back to headquarters to help in the Mara Gilmore investigation," Jackson said. "The other two, Parker and Brandie, are sticking around to provide you backup. I sent them outside to walk the perimeter. But I told them to be circumspect. We don't want to scare the guests any more than necessary. For now, it seems the danger is at bay."

"What did you learn from security?" Theo asked.

"The hotel videos are a wash," Jackson said. "They have cameras in the hallways. Only you three went in or out of the suite. The cameras on the grounds face away from the building. None are pointed at the presidential suite balcony. And there have been no reports of anyone suspicious climbing up to the third floor."

Theo ground his teeth. "That doesn't mean the bomber didn't climb up and set the bomb." The bomber was sneaky and far too clever. But nothing was going to keep Theo from protecting Willow.

"I talked to Donovan this morning," Jackson told them, keeping his voice low. "I'm being reassigned."

"Something to do with Mara?" Willow asked.

Theo could see the hope warring with dread in her eyes, and he wished there was some way to offer comfort. But until Mara Gilmore either turned herself in or was found, there would be no comfort to be had.

"No, this has nothing to do with Mara," Jackson replied. "I'm being tapped because of my former life as a US marshal. A woman I once protected is here in the park, and the marshals asked for my help. The woman she testified against has escaped from prison, and the powers that be suspect she's coming after her."

There was something in his tone, a note of anxiety that seemed a bit out of place. Had there been something between him and his protectee? "What is she doing in the park?" Willow asked.

"She's a doctoral student doing research on the black bears of the Olympic National Forest," Jackson said. "With a bomber running around and an escaped convict out to get her, Donovan agreed to let me help. Hopefully, our cases won't intersect. But if you need any more backup, call in Asher or Ruby."

Speaking of Ruby... "Do you know if Ruby and Eli Ballard are dating? I saw them together the other day," Willow said.

Jackson shrugged. "I haven't heard anything." He checked his watch. "I have to get a move on. You two stay safe."

"We will," Theo assured him. God willing. "You stay safe as well."

The next day arrived way too early for Willow. She'd had a horrible night's sleep, tossing and turning, starting at every noise. She hadn't realized how quiet the presidential suite had been.

The adjoining room doors had been cracked open. No noise emanated from the other room. She wondered if Theo had found any rest.

Star stirred on her bed under the window. There was no balcony on these rooms.

After refreshing Star's water bowl and then getting herself ready for the day, Willow knocked on the adjoining door. It opened, and Theo stood there dressed in jeans and a long-sleeve shirt. He'd shaved, and his hair was still damp and curling at the ends. So handsome he took her breath away. She forced back her attraction and strove for all business.

"After we get something to eat, I'd like to patrol the proposed all-terrain vehicle route. The bomber wants me out of the way so he can go back to destroying the trail. We need to stop him."

Theo's mouth quirked. "I had a feeling you'd plan to do that today. I talked to Donovan last night, and he isn't ready to pull you off this case."

A cascade of emotions passed through Willow. Anger at his audacity had her fisting her hands. "You called my boss?"

"No," Theo stated carefully. "He called me.

He wanted an update. I gave him my unvarnished opinion."

She could just imagine what Theo had said. She was grateful Donovan wasn't removing her. The desire to gloat was strong, but she held it in check.

"Donovan also asked about my thoughts regarding Mara Gilmore," Theo said.

"And?" Willow wanted to know what he thought as well.

"From everything I've read, Mara is bright and has no prior history of violence to suggest she's capable of a double homicide, but—"

Willow held up her hand. "Don't say it." She didn't want him to tell her that just because a person hadn't exhibited homicidal tendencies, that didn't mean they wouldn't kill if pushed far enough. Mara hadn't snapped. Willow refused to believe it.

"I know you want to believe in your friend's innocence, but an innocent person doesn't run and hide," Theo said.

"They would if they are afraid of something more than the police," Willow countered, thinking of Brandie's hypothesis that Mara was being forced to run.

"Then we need to pray the police find her before whoever else she's afraid of does," Theo said.

Anxiety twisted in Willow's chest, and she sent up a prayer for Mara.

Thirty minutes later, Willow, Star and Theo were downstairs at the restaurant. After a quick meal that satisfied her hunger, Willow and Star led the way into the forest. Rather than going toward the felled tree, they headed deeper into the thick woods. Theo stayed next to Willow and Star, while Parker and Brandie hung back, bringing up the rear.

"Have you given any thought to counseling?" Willow asked in a hushed tone so that Parker and Brandie wouldn't hear their conversation. She didn't need to air their marital issues to the candidates. She'd sensed a shift in Theo ever since he'd finally told her the truth of why he'd been pushing her away for the past year.

"Some," came Theo's noncommittal reply.

Aggravation chomped down hard on Willow. The man could be so stubborn and thick-headed. Didn't he want to be part of his child's life? She wasn't joking when she'd said she couldn't have Theo around their child if he continued down his self-destructive path. It broke her heart to know he'd crushed their love because of misplaced guilt and shame.

Was their love crushed? Or only lying dormant, waiting for a new chance to grow? She didn't know and couldn't begin to contemplate tending to it until Theo sought help.

Star's search proved unfruitful. They found no signs of any devices. Though they passed several people on the trail, Star didn't alert. Willow made sure to warn the hikers they passed to be careful and report any suspicious activity.

As they headed back toward the lodge, Willow's phone dinged with an incoming text.

The noise raised the hairs on the back of her neck, and her heart slammed into her throat. She'd come to dread that sound.

She recognized the number as being the one that had sent them to the hot springs with a fake threat. "It's him."

She swiped sideways, opening the text.

You were warned.

Urgent anxiety ricocheted through Willow's veins. "He's planning something. We have to stop him."

"Where?" Brandie said. "This park is so big."

"We should separate to search a wider area," Parker suggested.

Theo shook his head. "We're not separating. We'll alert the park rangers and the state patrol."

He took out his phone, but before he could dial, Willow's phone rang in her hand. She jumped at the sound. Was the bomber calling her? It wasn't the same number as the text sender, but it wasn't one from her contact list.

Steeling herself for something bad, she answered, putting the call on speaker. "Officer Bates."

"This is Ranger Kathleen Smith with the National Park Service," the female ranger's voice rang out. "You said for us to call you if we had any information about the bomber terrorizing the park."

Willow met Theo's gaze and saw the same grim dread in his eyes that she suffered deep in her gut. "Yes, Kathleen. What's happened?"

"We received an anonymous tip reporting a suspicious box left under a bench near the tide pools at Kalaloch Beach 4. We're headed there now, but we thought we should tell you."

Heart racing, Willow said, "Thank you, Kathleen. Secure the area, but stay back. We'll see you there."

"Are the tide pools on the route?" Parker asked.

Willow quickly spread out the map Ranger Steve had given her and found the tide pools at the end of the proposed trail. "Yes. This is where the trail will end."

She could only pray they reached the tide pools in time, before anyone was hurt.

The drive from the park entrance at Port Angeles where the Stark Lodge was located to the Kalaloch Beach tide pools on the Pacific coast took longer than Willow would have wanted. Lots of people were out and about on this beautiful June day, making the traffic thick. Theo parked in the public parking area, Parker and Brandie pulling up beside them.

They made their way to where several benches lined the bluff overlooking the water and empty beach. Differing bands of sediment and rocks where the bluffs met the beach provided lots of visual interest, along with the tide pools filled with sea life. Wind whipped off the ocean, and the briny scent of salt water filled Willow's senses as she led Star to where Park Ranger Kathleen and Park Ranger Mitch waited.

"We didn't want to touch it." Kathleen pointed to a small brown box sitting beneath a bench. "But we evacuated the area."

"We should wait for the state patrol's bomb tech," Theo said.

"Let Star work," Willow insisted. She and Star moved to the bench. "Search."

Star's nose went to the ground. She sniffed the box, sniffed the bench and then continued on moving away from the box, searching for a scent. Confused, Willow redirected Star back to the box. She sniffed it several times, looked at Willow and then moved away, completely uninterested.

"She's not alerting. I don't know what's in that box, but it's not an explosive or a weapon," Willow said in relief.

Theo stepped forward and squatted down to inspect the box.

Willow's breath caught. "It could be booby-trapped. We should wait."

He glanced up at her with an arched eyebrow. "Now you want to wait? I trust Star's nose. Don't you?"

She frowned, unwilling to admit she was concerned for his safety despite the confidence she had in her partner. "Of course I do. But why would someone leave a box here?"

"We're about to find out." He carefully lifted the box off the ground.

Willow's breath held in her chest. Nothing happened. Still, she couldn't exhale completely.

Theo set the box on the bench and pulled

a folding knife from the pocket of his windbreaker.

"Be careful," Willow couldn't help saying.

Using the knife, Theo cut through the tape holding the lid closed. When he flipped the lid back, he stared at the contents. The thunderous anger on his face had Willow moving forward to peer over his shoulder.

Inside was a small, square note with one word written in bold, black letters.

BOOM!

"This is some kind of joke," Parker said.

"A sick one," Brandie said.

A loud explosion from deep within the forest jolted Willow's heart into her throat. The ground shuddered. Black smoke rose in the distance, a dark plume against the blue sky.

"The box was a diversion."

The anger vibrating in Theo's voice matched the emotion filling Willow's chest. "He's taunting us."

After bagging the box and note, they left the beach and had no trouble following the trail of smoke to where another trailhead marker in the Hoh Rain Forest had been destroyed. Only this time the crater left behind was deep and wide enough to make the trail impassable, but thankfully no one had been hurt.

Leaving the scene in the hands of the crime scene unit and the park rangers, Willow and Theo and the candidates returned to the Stark Lodge. As a precaution, Willow had Star search her and Theo's rooms and breathed a sigh of relief when the dog didn't alert.

Willow's phone rang. She tensed, apprehension gripping her insides. Theo moved to stand next to her, his steady presence more comforting than she cared to admit. She blew out a breath when she saw that the number belonged to Bartholomew from the PNK9 unit's forensic team. "Hi, Bartholomew."

"Hello, Willow. I wanted to let you know we found a partial print on the blasting cap that you found. I ran it through every database I could think of, and it matches an old file."

Her breath caught. "One of my cases?"

"No. This is from a police report back twenty years ago. A young man named Charles Zimmer was questioned in connection to an arson case."

"Zimmer?" The name clanged through Willow's head. Her world tilted, and she gripped the edge of the door frame. Theo's arms snaked around her, and he held her steady. She leaned against his chest. Her breathing turned shallow.

"What's wrong?" Theo asked.

"Willow?" Bartholomew's concerned voice came through the phone.

To both men, she said, "The man who died in the blast that killed my father was named Wayne Zimmer."

Was Charles Zimmer a relation? And was he the bomber terrorizing the park and threatening Willow?

TEN

The memory of charred wood and disrupted dirt filled Willow's senses as her mind reeled to make sense of what she'd just been told.

Charles Zimmer. The son of the man who had been killed along with her father in a bombing that was never claimed by any organization and the murderer never found.

Charles Zimmer was their current bomber?

Unnerved by this connection to her past, Willow stared at Theo. "Are we really going to believe that Charles Zimmer is our ecoterrorist? He would've been eighteen when our fathers were killed. Why would he want to hurt the park? To hurt me?"

"The person who placed the bomb in the kiosk that killed your father and Wayne Zimmer that summer is still at large. It's not out of the realm of possibilities that Charles set that explosive device," Theo said. "Maybe his father figured it out and was trying to protect your father."

Willow's heart thudded in her chest. "We need to find Charles to determine if he's an ecoterrorist. And if so, is he targeting me because of my job or because of my father's death?"

From the phone still in her hand, Bartholomew's voice filled the space between her and Theo. "I'm sending you the last known address of Charles Zimmer. As well as the last DMV photo taken of him. The picture is from over six years ago, but it's the best we've got. I'm going to update Donovan as soon as he returns. He's out on a call."

Willow's phone dinged with two incoming texts. "Thank you, Bartholomew. I appreciate the work you do."

"Always happy to serve," Bartholomew replied before disconnecting.

Willow opened the texts to find the address of the Zimmer family was in Forks, Washington. A good hour-and-half drive on Highway 101 from where they were at the Stark Lodge near Port Angeles.

The second text showed a photo of a heavyset, Caucasian male wearing thick, black-framed glasses and with a dark mustache and goatee that emphasized his jowls. His dark hair was cut very short and combed flat against his head.

"I don't recognize him," Willow said. "We need to drive to Forks." She moved to prepare herself and Star. "I'm going to have the candidates stay here to be on alert in case the bomber, whether it's Charles or not, sets off another device."

Without hesitation, Theo grabbed the SUV keys from the top of the hotel dresser. "I'm ready to roll when you are."

The small town of Forks, Washington, sat between the Olympic Mountains and the Pacific Ocean on a prairie, but it was surrounded by dense rain forest. The winding highway could be treacherous in winter with nothing but trees on both sides. Theo was thankful for the relatively dry summer air as he drove the PNK9 SUV. Traveling down the main drag, Theo had a sense of being in a place time had forgotten. Squat, square buildings lined the street, and the businesses hadn't changed since they'd been built several decades ago.

Following the map directions to the address Bartholomew had sent Willow, Theo felt his pulse thrum with the knowledge this nightmare could soon be over. They just needed to find Charles Zimmer. Could he be the bomber?

There really could be no other explanation. His fingerprint had been found on the blasting cap near the site of the felled tree that nearly crushed Willow, the baby and Star. A deep-seated anger percolated in Theo's gut.

Beside him in the passenger seat, Willow drummed her fingers on the door handle. A new nervous habit. When had she allowed anxiety to manifest in a physical action?

Remorse for having been so deep in his own wallowing that he'd neglected to care for his wife swamped him. He held it at bay. He needed to stay focused and make sure Willow and the baby stayed safe. His mind strategized ways to approach Charles Zimmer.

The options were many. They could keep it friendly, just doing some groundwork on Willow's and Charles's fathers' murders. Following up on information about the old arson case in which Charles was a suspect.

But Theo decided the best way would be straightforward, confronting Charles outright on the recent bombings and catching him off guard.

Theo turned down a quiet residential street and pulled up in front of the Zimmer house, a disheveled-looking one-level home with moss growing on the roof and weeds overrunning the yard. "Whatever happened to Mrs. Zimmer?"

"I assumed she'd be here," Willow said, wrinkling her nose as she stared out the front window at the home.

"Well, if she is here, she's let the place go. It's shoddy," he said.

"Be nice—our child is listening."

He chuckled at the mild scolding tone as much as the words, even as his heart swelled with tender emotions at her use of *our child*. He was amazed how much the idea of having a little one who looked like Willow appealed to him. A sweet girl with big blue eyes and a feisty attitude running around melting hearts and causing havoc. To that end, he reached into the back seat for two flak vests and handed one to Willow. Keeping her and their baby safe was paramount. "Put this on."

Without comment, she took the vest and slipped it on, velcroing the sides shut before she hopped out and went to Star's compartment. Willow secured Star's vest around her compact body and then released the dog, keep her close with the leash attached to the back of the vest.

As they approached the front door of the Zimmer home, Theo put his hand on Willow's shoulder, positioning her behind him. Star stayed at Willow's side. He rapped his knuckles on the door. The sound echoed through the house. All was quiet. No sounds of life from within the home.

Glancing around the neighborhood, he noticed the other homes had been built in the same era, but they were mostly well maintained. Only the Zimmer house was an eyesore, which the neighbors no doubt deplored. Movement in the yard next door on the right had Theo pivoting, his hand going to his holstered weapon. A man in his late eighties, wearing a button-down golf shirt and Bermuda shorts, shuffled into view, shielding his eyes from the June sun as he peered at them over the chain-link fence. Large hydrangea bushes grew through the linked openings, spilling onto the Zimmer property.

"Are you looking for Cathy?" the old man asked, his voice shaky with age but firm. He barely stood taller than the fence, his scalp shining bright beneath wispy white hair.

Willow stepped to the porch railing, putting on her best charming smile. One Theo knew she reserved for the elderly, children and dogs. And once upon a time for him.

A deep ache from within his heart had Theo yearning for her to turn that smile on him again. It had been over a year since she'd looked at him with kindness and love.

His conscience snorted. That wasn't true. In the beginning, when he was in a bad way mentally and emotionally, she'd tried. She'd been tender and supportive, coaxing him to open up. But he'd resisted. And again, recently, when he'd finally spilled his guts, she'd been kind and compassionate. Could there ever be a possibility that she might love him again?

The thought sent a tremor through him. He returned his attention to the present situation.

"Hello there," Willow said pleasantly and proceeded to introduce herself, Star and Theo. "And you are?"

"I'm Gerald Horton. You can call me Jerry." He eyed Star. "That's a good-looking dog. I had a chocolate Lab once. She was the best dog. I miss having a companion."

Willow patted Star and then gestured for her to lie down. Star found a shady spot. "Good to meet you, Jerry. We are looking for Mrs. Zimmer and her son, Charles. Would you happen to know when they'll be back?"

"Back?" Jerry said. "Cathy's not coming back. Least as far as I know. She moved to Florida. Said the rain was getting to her after all these years. I don't blame her. We have so few days here when we get a good dose of sunshine and not weeping clouds."

Weeping clouds. Theo liked that analogy. But today the sun was shining. And hope was beginning to take root deep in his soul. He gave himself a mental shake. He couldn't afford to be distracted. "What about Charles?"

Jerry gave a shrug. "He went off to college far away, from what I remember. Comes back every now and then."

"When did Cathy Zimmer move to Florida?" Willow asked.

"Well, I reckon it's been at least five years," Jerry said.

"This house has stood empty ever since?" Theo asked the old man.

"Most of the time. Though I have seen Charles coming and going. Usually late at night."

"Recently?" Willow asked.

"Off and on over the years," came Jerry's reply.

Theo mulled this over. Charles must live and work fairly close, or at least within the state. To

Willow, Theo said in a low tone, "We should do a wellness check. You never know."

He didn't really think they'd find Charles's dead body inside. More likely bomb-making material. However, Star wasn't alerting. But as excuses went, a wellness check was right up there among the best.

Willow gave a nod. To the neighbor she said, "Thank you for your help, Jerry."

"Did Charles do something bad?" Jerry moved closer to the fence.

The question slid a cold fist into Theo's gut. "Why would you ask?"

"Charles was always getting into trouble after his daddy was murdered. Years back, Charles was suspected of burning down the grange hall. They could never prove it. But I heard him and his mama arguing about it."

"Why would Charles want to burn down the hall?"

"There was some sort of meeting taking place. An environmental group. Charles blamed his father's death on those people."

"Do you remember the name of the group?" Willow asked.

"Freedom Forest Fighters," Jerry said. "I think. It's been over twenty years ago now."

Theo said beneath his breath, "You ever heard of this group?"

"It sounds vaguely familiar," Willow stated, her eyebrows drawn together. "I was thirteen when this all happened. My whole world literally exploded that day."

To the neighbor, Theo said, "We appreciate you taking the time to talk to us. We're going to do a wellness check on Charles, just to make sure nothing has happened to him." He figured it was best to head off any questions as to why they were breaking in the door.

The old man's eyes widened. "You think Charles could be dead? Inside the house?"

"We hope not, sir," Willow told him. "But we can't seem to locate him. Best to be safe."

Jerry scratched his head. "Should I reach out to his mom? She did leave a number."

"He could've told us that to begin with," Theo growled beneath his breath. Louder, he said, "No, thank you, Jerry. But we will take that number. Would you mind writing it down? We'll grab it from you before we leave."

"Of course, I can do that." Jerry shuffled away toward the back of his house.

Theo and Willow faced the front door again.

"We better let Star search the grounds to see

if the house is rigged with explosives," Willow said. "So far she is not alerting."

Theo nodded. "Let's take a walk around the premises."

Willow clucked into her cheek, and Star jumped to her feet. Theo led the way down off the front porch but moved aside when Willow and Star nudged him. He kept a tight visual on the pair and the house as Star sniffed at the foundation, the air vents and the air-conditioning unit in the backyard.

Star gave no indication of explosives or weapons on the premises. That didn't mean there couldn't be some inside. Just not within close proximity to the outer edges of the house. At least, Theo would go inside on that premise, making sure that he and Willow were both alert and prepared.

Back at the front door, Willow asked, "Do you want to do the honors?"

"You mean kick in the door, obviously." He stepped back, preparing to do just that.

Willow halted him with a hand on his forearm. "No." She produced a small zippered case from the utility belt around her waist. "I meant pick the lock."

Theo made a face. "That's no fun."

Her mouth curved. "But better on the department's budget. I don't know about you FBI agents, but PNK9 must watch our pennies. Getting a locksmith out here might take a while. Plus, the way you operate, we'd have to provide a whole new door."

"Hey, now." He liked how she teased him. "I do resemble that."

She smirked. "The first step is to admit it."

He barked out a laugh and arched an eyebrow.

She waved the lock-picking tools in his face. "Me or you?"

His hand closed over the lock-picking kit and her hand, the skin soft beneath his touch. "Me."

Slowly, he took the kit from her and unzipped it. He took out two little tension tools before kneeling in front of the lock on the door. He sent up a prayer heavenward that the lock he was about to pick hadn't been booby-trapped. There were other ways to maim or hurt besides explosives and weapons. Acid came to mind.

Quickly, he pulled out a set of latex gloves from his pocket, hoping the thin material would be enough of a barrier if needed. He went to work. Willow had taught him years ago how to pick a lock. It wasn't exactly a skill the FBI employed often. Not when they had a badge that usually opened doors.

Finally, he heard the lock give. He stilled, waiting for something, anything, to happen, and when nothing did, he stood. Returning the little tools to the kit, he handed them back to Willow.

"One minute, five seconds," she said.

He tucked in his chin. "You were timing me?"

"Always good to know how you can improve."

The easy banter, so familiar and welcome, released some of the tension from his shoulders. Old feelings sprouted, and he tamped them down, not willing to let anything distract him, even his lovely wife. He readied himself with one hand on his holstered weapon and the other going to the knob. "Stay behind me."

Rather than answering him verbally, Willow reeled Star close, and they stepped behind Theo. He indulged in a small smile as his hand gripped the doorknob and twisted. Again, he waited, wondering what would greet them on the other side of the door.

He pushed open the door. A musty odor emanated from within.

"Stinks," he muttered.

Willow stepped closer, taking a deep, audible sniff. "I don't smell decay."

A good sign that neither of them could smell

the stench of death from within the house. He looked along the threshold of the door for trip wires. He didn't see any, but that didn't mean there couldn't be some. He withdrew his weapon and flashlight from his belt, shining the light on the floor. Relatively sure there wasn't a wire strung across the entrance, he stepped inside. The heel of his hiking boot made a barely audible sound on the hardwood floor.

Willow touched his elbow. He stepped to the side of the door so that she and Star could come into the house. Willow unhooked Star from the leash and gave the dog the search command. The dog trotted off, nose in the air and then to the floor. Star searched the corners, sniffing along the floorboards and down the hall, disappearing into one room after another before circling through the kitchen and returning to Willow's side.

Willow gave Star a treat. "Good girl." To Theo, Willow said, "House appears clean."

Returning his weapon to his holster, Theo walked all the way inside, noting it was like stepping back in time. The furniture screamed 1980s. Probably when the Zimmers bought the home. A thick layer of dust coated every surface. Willow headed down the hall while Theo stepped into the kitchen. The refrigerator gurgled. Inside was a half a gallon of milk, the expiration date a week out. A box of cereal sat on the counter, and a bowl with a spoon had been left in the sink. Footprints in the dust on the floor indicated a large boot.

"What do you make of these?" he asked Willow as she joined him. He pointed to the footprints—every other one was scuffed, as if Charles, assuming it was Charles, dragged his feet.

"Maybe he has some neuropathy going with his feet," Willow said. "There's three bedrooms and one bath. Charles's room is down the hall. Come see."

Theo followed her down the hall, past a gallery of family photos hanging on the walls. He stopped to examine them. Willow stopped next to him.

"That's Wayne Zimmer. I recognize him from that day. He was arguing with my dad. I don't know what was said. I don't know if he was trying to prevent my father from going near the kiosk or what."

"This must be Charles," Theo said, tapping the framed glass photo.

A dark mop of hair hung over the boy's eyes. He looked like any normal teenager nearing puberty. Empathy squeezed Theo's chest. For whatever reason, Charles had lost his father. But it didn't explain why he was running around the forest or trying to hurt Willow. If he was indeed their suspect. Was he hoping to stop the all-terrain vehicle trail, as they theorized? Or did he just want to blow things up and had decided to target the woods?

Charles's bedroom was neat and tidy. The twin bed had been made, and there was no dust anywhere on the dresser or desk, where a stack of old textbooks took up space.

"There's clothes in the closet and the dresser," Willow said.

Further proof that Charles did return to his childhood home. But where was he when not visiting the house?

"The master bedroom and the sewing room are undisturbed." Willow gestured to the other rooms. "No footprints. Charles didn't go into them."

"Let's go get that number from the neighbor." Theo headed back down the hall. "This house gives me the creeps."

They hurriedly left the house, locking the door behind them. "You know he's going to realize somebody's been inside when he sees all our footsteps in the dust."

"Small price to pay," Theo said. "Besides, I've a feeling that the neighbor, Jerry, will inform him of our interest if we don't find Charles first."

"I think you're right." By the time they made it down the sidewalk to the front door of the neighbor, the old man had the door open and was waiting with a piece of paper held out.

"Here's Cathy's number in Florida."

"Thank you, Jerry." Willow handed the man her card. "You call me if you see anything suspicious or you have any inkling of trouble."

Theo grimaced. Another person with her cell phone number.

"I appreciate your service, ma'am," Jerry said, pocketing the card.

Snagging Willow by the elbow, Theo said, "We've got to get going. You have a nice day, Mr. Horton."

The old man nodded and shuffled backward, shutting his door.

"We have a couple of new leads," Theo said. "We'll find out more about this group Charles tried to burn down. See if there's a connection to your father's death."

"I want to have a conversation with Cathy Zimmer," Willow said. "I'll try her in the morning."

On the way out of Forks, they stopped at a drive-through diner. Willow ordered a turkey burger with the works, while he ordered a good old-fashioned hamburger with cheese and mushrooms. After eating, they hit the road.

The sun began its descent in the west, creating long shadows from the towering hemlock and cedars dotting both sides of the winding highway. Sunlight dappled in and out of view, giving Theo a pounding headache. Willow had long since donned a pair of sunglasses from her pack. He hadn't thought to stick a pair in his pocket before leaving the lodge.

Willow dug through the glove box and produced a pair of women's sunglasses. "I knew there had to be a pair in here." She handed them to Theo.

With one hand on the steering wheel, he used the other to put on the square, rhinestone-bedazzled glasses. The darkened lens provided a bit of relief. "It takes a real man to wear women's glasses."

"Well, if I see a real man, I'll let you know," Willow quipped.

He slanted her a glance to see her cheeky smile. His heart bumped. "I was thinking when we returned to the hotel—"

A light bouncing off a bumper in the rearview mirror distracted him. Where had the big truck come from? He didn't remember it being back there. He was right on their bumper. Crowding them. Theo looked down at the speedometer. He was going ten miles over the speed limit. He pushed the needle up another five clicks. Still, the guy stayed on his bumper.

"What's this jerk doing?" Theo groused. A sudden sinking sensation in his gut had him warning Willow. "Brace yourself. I think this guy is trying to—"

Before he could finish his sentence, the truck slammed into the back of their PNK9 Unit vehicle.

ELEVEN

Metal against metal screeched as the over-size silver pickup truck rammed into the back of the SUV. The steering wheel jerked within Theo's grasp, and he fought to keep the tires pointed straight. He needed to get out of the path of this truck. He couldn't make out the driver. The guy had the sun visor down and the sun was glaring off his windshield, reflecting in the rearview mirror. Theo moved the SUV over into the left, into the oncoming traffic lane, and the truck followed him.

"Theo, tell me you have this," Willow demanded, her hands gripping the dashboard.

Everything inside Theo thundered with rage. He was not going to let this creep in the truck be the end of him and his family. "Willow, hang on."

Theo jerked the wheel, sending the SUV back into the right lane. He then slammed on the brakes before the big, four-wheel-drive truck could also change lanes behind them. The truck zoomed past in the left lane, its brake lights burning bright red as the driver brought the vehicle to a crawl.

"Theo!"

An oncoming semitruck, carrying a load of timber, rounded the corner, heading straight for the pickup truck sitting in the oncoming traffic lane. The semitruck's horn blared.

Theo pulled the SUV to the side, hugging the edge of the road in anticipation of the semi plowing into the smaller truck.

The guy in the pickup truck reversed and zoomed past Theo and Willow.

Theo tried to make out the driver's face, but he was wearing a hoodie, baseball hat and dark sunglasses.

Twisting in his seat, Theo watched the pickup truck do a 180-degree turn, step on the gas and speed away, averting disaster with only seconds to spare. The semitruck slowed down enough to keep from hitting the back end of the smaller truck.

Another horn honked. Theo realized cars were stacking up behind him. He put the SUV in Drive and hit the gas. His heart revved along with the engine.

"Were you able to make out the license plate number?" Willow asked, her voice shaky.

"Negative. He'd smeared them with mud." Theo's heart played a heavy metal concert in his chest. He didn't even like heavy metal music. But the clanging and banging wouldn't stop. "There was something…"

"What?"

An image filtered into his brain and out again, lightning fast. He couldn't grasp it. All he could think was he and his family could easily have died today.

He called the local police and reported the assault, giving them the truck's description.

Because there was nothing more to be done, he started driving again but kept a watchful eye in all directions in case of another attack.

Breathing out a sigh of relief when he pulled into the parking lot at the Stark Lodge, Theo put the SUV in Park and gripped the steering wheel. For a long moment, neither he nor Willow moved. He was shaken to his core. He had been in hairier situations, but the stakes had never been as high.

He turned to stare at Willow, her beautiful face coming starkly into focus. Her light brown hair was pulled back in a low ponytail, but tendrils had escaped to curl around her face. Her blue eyes were wide, and she had one hand over her abdomen, a protective gesture that scored through him.

With everything inside him, Theo wanted to draw her close and tell her it would be okay. Tell her he would take care of her and their child. He would protect them. But he knew he hadn't earned that right yet.

Regret for having pushed her away instead of clinging to her in his darkest moments made him wish there was a rewind button he could push. So he could go back and do things differently. Affection and care for this admirable and strong woman sprouted from the dregs of his heart.

Could they recapture what they once had? Would Willow ever forgive him? Could he ever forgive himself?

He wasn't sure how to proceed. He only knew he had to do everything in his power to keep Willow and the baby safe.

"Have dinner with me." His voice echoed inside the SUV.

From the special compartment in the back, Star whined, clearly impatient to be let out.

Willow slowly turned her gaze, focusing on his face. Confusion knitted her brow. "Dinner?"

"We have to decompress," he told her. He knew how important it was to take a beat after a harrowing, adrenaline-filled moment. "We don't have a common room anymore. So have dinner with me in the lodge's restaurant. On the back patio. It's a beautiful night."

"I don't know that I can eat—"

"Yes, you can. You have to eat. You have to keep up your strength for you and the baby."

She nodded as if she understood, but she still looked dazed.

Worry gnawed through him. He popped open his door and climbed out, hustling around to her side of the vehicle. He half expected her to already be out by the time he reached for her door handle, instead she sat there, just staring straight ahead. Maybe she was more traumatized than he realized. Concern itched his skin. He opened her door and reached for her hand.

She clung to him, her fingers tightening around his. He helped her out of the vehicle. Her legs wobbled. He circled his arms around her, and she melted into him, laying her cheek against his chest. For a long moment, they stood there, not saying a word, just letting their hearts beat together.

The clearing of a throat broke them apart.

On a rush of adrenaline and instinct, Theo spun, keeping Willow between himself and the passenger door, where she was out of sight.

He blew out a breath at the sight of Parker and Brandie standing there.

"Sorry to interrupt," Parker said, his voice laced with something between amusement and disapproval. "We oversaw the installation of some new security measures for the lodge."

Willow stepped around Theo, shooting him a censuring look before smiling at the candidates. "Good job, you two."

She'd apparently regained her composure and clearly took issue with his protectiveness. He couldn't help it, but he refrained from voicing his thoughts.

"Take the night off," Willow continued. "I think we've all earned it."

"Is everything okay?" asked Brandie, her gaze assessing. "What happened to your vehicle?"

Theo grimaced at the crunched bumper but was thankful the hit hadn't been worse.

"We had a bit of trouble, but we're good," Willow told the younger officer. "We're going to grab some dinner."

Theo was glad to hear Willow say *they* were going to eat. But first, he needed to shower and change. Sweat beaded on his back from the adrenaline, and grime from the Zimmer house coated his skin. And he wanted time to make arrangements with the restaurant.

He and Willow said goodbye to Parker and Brandie, letting the two young officers loose for the evening.

When they reached their hotel rooms, Theo said, "I'll meet you downstairs in forty minutes."

Willow's gaze searched his face. "I'll be there," she promised.

After making sure both of their doors and windows were locked and there was no one hiding under the bed or in the closets, Theo retreated to his room, shutting the adjoining doors. He had work to do and a lot to make up for with Willow. He'd better get started.

Willow fussed with her hair, wondering why she was taking so much care in her appearance when she was just going downstairs to the restaurant to have dinner with Theo. It was no big deal. Only, somehow, she sensed it was a big deal. Her nerves jangled along her limbs, and she chalked her nervousness up to the incident on the road. The person in the pickup truck had been intent on making them crash. Only Theo's expert driving kept them from harm.

It upset her that they hadn't found Charles Zimmer.

Willow retrieved the piece of paper that Jerry Horton had given her with Cathy Zimmer's phone number. Despite the late hour, considering the time zone difference, she dialed. The call rang and rang. Strange that it didn't go to voice mail. With technology today, even a landline had digital voice mail.

Willow's next call was to Jasmin. After greeting the other woman, Willow said, "I need you to verify a phone number for me." She read off the number on the paper. "It should belong to a Cathy Zimmer."

"One second." Jasmin placed Willow on hold.

Willow scratched Star behind the ears as she waited.

"It sure does," Jasmin said when she came back on the line. "You want me to ring her?"

"I've tried, with no answer. Do me a favor and have the local PD there do a wellness check on her."

"On it," Jasmin said before hanging up. Glancing at the time, Willow hurriedly applied lip gloss, then chided herself for the effort. She secured her weapon and badge in a small purse that she'd packed as an afterthought when she'd left home. As she and Star rushed from the room, she had to admit to herself that Theo had been a bit different since their talk the other night, more like his old self. This latest attempt on their lives had affected them both deeply. Was he softening? Would he agree to counseling? She decided she would bring it up again at dinner.

She didn't dare let herself hope or even entertain any tender emotions. She could be hurt in the end if Theo decided to hang onto his despair rather than doing whatever was necessary to make himself healthy and whole. She would have to stay guarded, because she had to do right by her child.

Willow found Theo sitting at a table in the far corner of the patio, away from any of the other guests. He'd told her to bring Star, and now she understood why. He'd made arrangements for them to have their own private little area, where Star could be with them undisturbed.

The table was set up for two with candles and glasses filled with sparkling apple cider. Breadsticks sat in a basket on the table, and her stomach grumbled. Theo stood as she approached. He looked good. He'd changed into khaki pants and a long-sleeve blue button-down shirt that looked so good against his sun-kissed face. He'd swept his dark brown hair back in a style that just begged for her to run her fingers through the strands. He'd shaved again, his skin looking smooth and kissable.

She reminded herself to stay guarded, but

she wanted to enjoy this night. She wanted this moment of downtime. If only they could erase the past and start again.

Soft jazz music played from speakers, creating a sweet and romantic scene.

Theo held out her chair. She sat, and his hands drifted up to her shoulders and lingered briefly, his touch light and warm.

"You're beautiful," he murmured.

Suddenly she was glad she'd opted to wear the flowered sundress that swirled around her knees and the lightweight, pale pink sweater she'd thrown into her suitcase at the last moment. "Thank you."

Star lay down at her feet.

"I hope it's okay I ordered salads and appetizers," he said as he sat across from her. "I figured you could decide your own main dish. But I thought we should probably get some food in our systems right away."

She appreciated his thoughtfulness.

This seemed like a date. A date with her husband. For some reason, she couldn't bring herself to remember that he'd soon be her ex-husband. Tonight, she wanted to forget about their crumbling marriage. She wanted to forget about the awful year they'd had. "You always do know how to treat me well," she said.

"I haven't done a very good job of that this

last year," he said. "I hope you know it was never about you."

"I do, now," she replied. "Let's put that on the back burner tonight." She picked up a breadstick and held it out like a sword. He grinned and picked up his own breadstick, and they tapped the bread together as if they were the finest crystal goblets ever made.

"Bon appétit," she murmured.

"Salut," he replied with a faint smile.

The familiar gesture warmed her heart, and she settled in. Soon garden salads and mini raviolis smothered in Alfredo sauce arrived at the table. They gave the waitress their main course orders and dug into their food. They talked of past adventures, like hiking through Peru and skiing in Aspen during their vacations. They talked of politics, debating the latest issues. They talked about anything and everything but the one topic that they needed to discuss: the future.

Just as they were finishing their meal, a guitarist and vocalist stepped onto the small stage that had been set up at the back of the patio. The woman's voice enchanted as she crooned a love song, and the guitarist's fingers moved skillfully on the strings. From their vantage point in the corner, they could watch the crowd, who sat with rapt attention watching the performers. Soon people were up dancing in front of the stage. A nostalgic ache throbbed in Willow's heart. It had been so long since she'd danced with Theo.

After their plates had been cleared away and the dessert order put in, Theo stood and reached out. "Dance with me."

She hesitated. "What about Star?"

Theo smiled, his gaze tender. "We'll dance right here. We don't need to be front and center."

Placing her hand in his, she allowed him to pull her to her feet and straight into his arms. His touch was sure and familiar yet as thrilling as if this were their first date.

"Do you remember the first time we came close to dancing?" he murmured in her ear.

She inhaled the masculine scent of his aftershave. Placing her hands on his shoulders, she leaned back and gazed into his face. "It was our first case together. We had the suspect cornered. We each came at him from a different direction, and we collided."

"And we took him down," Theo said. "And then I spun you like this."

He took her hand in his and, with a precise move, spun her out so that she stretched arm's length away, and then with a gentle tug, she twirled back into his arms.

She laughed at the memory and at the feelings crowding her chest. Affection, hope and delight. And trepidation.

Then Star was there, wedging herself between them.

Willow laughed. "Just like last time." Only then, the dog had planted her feet on the suspect's chest and bared her teeth.

Theo chuckled. "She doesn't like to be left out."

"Or she's being protective," Willow teased.

"I bought that the first time," Theo said. "This time, however, I think it's FOMO."

"You could be right," she agreed. Star did at times have a case of the fear of missing out.

The song ended, and they returned to their seats. Star settled back down next to Willow's chair.

Theo raised an eyebrow.

She shrugged. "What can I say? She loves me."

Willow had the sudden yearning to hear those words from her husband. She took a breath and slowly let it out. Those words might never be said again between them. But that didn't mean she was willing to give up completely. "About counseling…"

Theo's expression shuttered. He leaned back in the chair. "You're like a dog with a bone," he groused. "You have to give me time. I'm not willing—ready—to commit to..."

Disappointment flooded her veins. She'd hoped he'd seen that doing the hard thing was worth it for her and the baby. But apparently not. "How long should I give you?"

He sat forward, earnestness shining in his eyes. "Can't we just work this out between us?"

"This isn't an *us* thing," she said. She suspected his pride was at the root of his resistance. "It's not weakness to admit you need help. It's actually a sign of strength and humility to let someone else—"

"You're helping me," he interjected.

Her temper flared, but she held it in check. "I am not a counselor. I'm your wife. I can only do so much. You need to see a trained professional."

For a moment, he stared at her, then his gaze zipped away. "Maybe."

His reticence was like a dagger to her heart. She couldn't move forward with him, not like this. She wanted to press him for a commitment, but weariness pulled at her. Best to let him mull over the idea. Nothing could be accomplished tonight, anyway. It was time to call it an evening.

Her phone rang from inside her purse. She

stiffened, dread gripping her insides. Her gaze met Theo's, and she saw the same grim anticipation in his expression.

She tugged the phone out of her purse and looked at the number. "It's Donovan." She let out a breath, but the tension didn't ease. She hoped and prayed this wasn't something bad. "Hello?"

"Willow, I heard what happened to you and Theo today. I want you both here within the hour."

Surprise pulled Willow's mouth into a grimace. "Donovan, we can't drive there within an hour. Plus, it's late. We could be there in the morning."

"No, I'm sending the chopper," he said. "It should be there momentarily. I want an update, and I want it in person."

Theo nodded and signaled for the waitress.

"We'll see you soon." Willow hung up. "He sounds very agitated."

In the distance, the unmistakable sound of a helicopter growing closer filled the air.

Theo paid their bill and canceled their dessert order. They hurried to the front of the Stark Lodge. On the other side of the parking lot, there was a large stretch of meadow where the unit's helicopter set down. Theo helped Willow climb into the cabin, then lifted Star in after her. They each put on headsets as the bird lifted off the ground. Soon they were flying over the Olympic National Forest through the night sky toward the city of Olympia and the PNK9 Unit headquarters. Solving their marriage problems would have to wait. Work also seemed to come between them. But she had never dreamed their careers would be the cause of so much heartache.

TWELVE

Self-conscious in her summer dress and sandals, Willow walked with Theo and Star to the entrance of the large, two-story stone building housing the Pacific Northwest K9 Unit headquarters. She couldn't remember the last time she'd worn civilian clothes to a meeting with her boss.

Because it was night, the open desk area where the officers worked was dark save for the light spilling from Chief Donovan Fanelli's office. As she, Star and Theo proceeded into the belly of the building, motion-activated lights flickered on. Star eagerly entered the office, her tail wagging to see the chief.

Donovan rose from behind his desk and came around to kneel and scratch Star behind the ears. "How are you, girl?"

Donovan looked up at Willow. His gaze then moved to Theo. "Have a seat."

Willow exchanged a wary glance with Theo

before they each took a seat in the plush leather chairs facing Donovan's desk.

Donovan stood and hitched a hip on the edge of his desk. "I don't like this latest development." Folding his arms, he stared at Willow and Theo. "Charles Zimmer. The son of the man who was killed with your father. Is this some kind of personal vendetta Zimmer has against you? Does he blame your family for his father's death?"

Willow swallowed back the anxiety clawing up her throat. All good questions. But none of it made sense. "If our bomber is Charles Zimmer, I don't think this has anything to do with me. Why would Charles wait twenty years to come after me if his motivation was revenge for his father's death? My father died in that explosion. If anything, we should be kindred spirits. Not enemies."

"My guess," Theo said, "would be that Zimmer is protesting the all-terrain vehicle route. He may not even realize that the officer investigating the bombings is the daughter of the man who died with his father. Willow doesn't use her maiden name."

"This is true," Donovan said. "But that doesn't mean he couldn't somehow connect you to your father." He moved around the desk to sit in his captain's chair. He planted his elbows on the desk and steepled his fingers. "To be on the safe side, I'm pulling you from this case."

Willow sat on the edge of the seat. "Please don't. Star is the best bomb-detection dog in the unit. In the whole state." She might be exaggerating that last point, but she couldn't let the chief bench her. Not after they'd already come this far. "Let us continue to patrol the park. Every law enforcement agency in the state is out looking for Charles Zimmer. He'll turn up."

"That's the thing," Donovan said. "Charles Zimmer seems to have vanished. Outside of that address in Forks, there is no other place of residence on record. He is flying far under the radar. We don't even know if he looks like his last DMV photo. Six years is a long time."

"Now that we know who we are looking for," Theo said, "we have a better chance of stopping the park bomber. I sent Zimmer's photo to the FBI tech in DC. He's going to do an age progression on Zimmer's image and give us a few variables of what he might look like now."

Donovan lips pressed together. "I'm going to pull in more resources, as well. We're spread thin right now."

"All the more reason for Star and me to stay

on the job," Willow stated, desperate to plead her case. "We know the park better than anyone."

"You can be assured, I'll keep her safe," Theo interjected.

Donovan gave him a slow nod. "All right. I will let you two continue to work on this, but if there are any more incidents—"

"We understand," Theo said. "We won't take chances. If there's even a hint of danger, I'll get her and Star out."

Though Willow appreciated Theo's confidence, she had no illusions about how dangerous this assignment was. Her hand automatically went to her abdomen. Donovan's eyes flared, and she quickly removed her hand from her midsection.

"Is there something I should know?" Donovan said, his voice dropping an octave.

As much as Willow wanted to keep her pregnancy a secret until she and Theo had figured out what was happening with their marriage, she couldn't lie to the boss. If he found out later that she had kept this information from him, she would lose his trust. And that was not something she was willing to risk. "We are expecting."

A thundercloud swept over Donovan's features. "And you want to stay on this case?"

Theo reached across and took her hand, threading his fingers through hers. The show of support brought the burn of tears to the backs of her eyes. "I want her to. We're just past the first trimester. The doctor said there's no reason to worry."

"Unless, of course, this bomber, presumably Charles Zimmer, does you in." Donovan's voice held a sharp edge.

"We won't let that happen," Theo stated firmly.

Letting out a heavy breath, Donovan sat back. "Though congratulations are in order," he said, "I will hold off until this case is finished. You bring Charles Zimmer, or the bomber, if they aren't the same person, to justice. Then we will celebrate your victory and the new life you are bringing into this world."

"Thank you, sir," Willow said quickly.

Donovan gave her a sharp nod. Then he turned his gaze to Theo. "What is your assessment on Mara Gilmore?"

Willow inhaled at the change in topic. She was thankful to be out from under Donovan's spotlight, but she was concerned for her friend.

"As I explained to you the other night," Theo said. "It's very confusing. From all accounts, Mara was top of her class in the police academy as well as her forensic studies. Yet there are so many mistakes in this case that a top-notch forensic investigator would never make. I can't find anything in her file or in the testimony of her friends and family—" He slanted Willow a glance. "—that would lead me to believe she would do this."

"What do you make of her running away when Colt and Danica arrived at the murder scene?"

Willow's gut twisted. It was the question on everyone's mind.

"That is a puzzle," Theo said. "If she were innocent, why not go to her friends and colleagues, instead of fleeing the scene?"

"There's more to the story than appears on the surface," Willow insisted, but she couldn't keep the frustration from lacing her words. What was going on?

Donovan heaved a sigh. "I've got the state's attorney breathing down my neck. He wants closure on this case."

Curling her fingers, Willow said, "Shouldn't we want the truth?"

"Of course we want the truth," Donovan said, with a good dose of exasperation in his tone.

His desk phone rang.

He lifted the receiver. "Fanelli." He listened, his face paling and turning to granite. "I'll be right there."

He stood, retrieving his weapon and sticking it in the holster at his hip. "There's been a break-in at the training center."

Willow's heart jackknifed in her chest. "Is Peyton with the bloodhound pups? Are they okay?"

" I'm praying they're all okay." Donovan stomped out of the office. Willow, Theo and Star hurried after him. They wound their way through the darkened building as lights trailed in their wake. By the time they made it across the yard to the training center, ambulances, with sirens blaring and lights flashing, had arrived and roared to a halt.

Donovan directed the paramedics to where Jonathan, one of the trainers, lay unconscious on the ground with Peyton kneeling at his side.

Willow rushed to Peyton, drawing her out of the paramedics' way. "What happened?"

Peyton appeared on the brink of being sick. She swallowed convulsively before managing to say, "Someone knocked out Jonathan and stole the three puppies."

Willow sucked in a gasp. "Oh, no."

"Tell us everything that happened," Theo instructed.

Gulping back a sob, Peyton said, "Jonathan was giving the puppies a last chance to be outside before we kennel them for the night." She shuddered. "I heard a commotion and Jonathan yelling. By the time I got out here, he was laying on the ground." Distress pierced her voice. "And the puppies were gone."

"You didn't see the vehicle driving away?" Donovan's voice gentled.

"No." Peyton shook her head. "But I heard tires squealing on the pavement." She fisted her hands at her sides. "I should've come out with him."

"And probably you also would have been hurt in the process," Donovan said. "We will find the puppies."

"Peyton, why don't you sit down?" Theo said.

Sending him a grateful smile, Willow urged Peyton to a bench off to the side of the play yard.

Several Olympia police cruisers screeched to a halt in the parking lot, and officers descended on the scene.

Willow took her hands. "This isn't your fault."

"Poor Jonathan. They could have killed him." A sob escaped Peyton.

The paramedics loaded Jonathan onto a wheeled gurney and put him in the ambulance bay.

Peyton jumped to her feet. "I should go with him."

Donovan stepped up, halting her. "I'll go with him. You stay here and secure the rest of the dogs."

Peyton nodded, but Willow could tell she wasn't happy not to be going with the ambulance.

"We'll help you," Willow offered.

"There's not much left to do," Peyton told them. "Without the puppies here, I only have two other dogs I'm currently working with, and they're already settled for the night."

"Still, you shouldn't be alone right now," Willow insisted.

"I appreciate that," Peyton said. "Those poor puppies. They're newly trained in scent detection—they aren't pets."

"Worth a pretty penny, I would imagine," Theo said.

"They are, but only if they are needed for that work." Peyton led the way inside the training center. "Let me get Star some water."

Willow watched as Peyton busied herself rinsing out a bowl and filling it with cool water. She figured Peyton needed something to keep herself from thinking too much about the stolen puppies. It was a loss for them all.

As Star drank from the water bowl, Willow asked Theo, "Do you think someone took the puppies just for the money they would bring reselling them?"

"Hard to say," Theo said. "If someone knows how highly trained these dogs are and wanted to use them in an effort to thwart law enforcement... They might not be resold but used for illegal purposes instead."

"Where would they take them?" Peyton asked, worry underscoring her words.

"There's no telling," Theo said. "I'll alert my boss. The FBI can help in the search."

Theo stood and walked away to make the phone call.

Peyton squeezed Willow's hands. "I sensed tension between you two last time I saw you. Is everything okay between you?"

"It's better than it was," Willow admitted. Knowing the news of her pregnancy would be out soon, because there was no reason for Donovan to keep it a secret, Willow decided to confide in Peyton. "I'm pregnant."

Peyton gave a squeal of delight and pulled Willow into a hug. "That's wonderful!" She pulled back and peered into Willow's face. Her eyebrows drew together. "Isn't it?"

"Yes and no." Willow glanced over to where Theo paced while talking to his boss. "We have some issues to work out." Emotion clogged her throat. "I don't know if we'll be able to resolve them. I'm scared, Peyton. I don't know if we're going to make it."

"I have every confidence you and Theo will work this out," Peyton said. "Whatever it is. I know you love each other. I've seen it over the years. There can't be anything so bad that you can't overcome it."

As much as Willow wanted to believe what Peyton said was true, she couldn't let her friend's optimism gain a foothold. "I hope you're right," Willow told her. "But I just don't know if he's willing to do the hard work."

"I'll pray for you both," Peyton said.

"Thank you, my friend. I'd appreciate it."

Theo returned to say, "My boss is sending out an alert through the agency. He'll talk to Donovan and see if they can coordinate their efforts."

"Thank you both for being here," Peyton said. "Why are you here? I heard about the situation in the Olympic National Forest."

Willow quickly filled Peyton in on everything they knew about the serial bomber and Charles Zimmer.

"That's frightening," Peyton said. "Did you ever meet Charles Zimmer when you were young?"

Willow gave the question some thought. "I don't know. My mother and I went to Wayne Zimmer's funeral. But we didn't talk to anybody. I don't know if Cathy Zimmer and her son came to my father's funeral." Something Willow could ask her mother. "Maybe my mom would have some memory of meeting Cathy and Charles."

However, Willow didn't know how that would play into what was happening now. Twenty years was a long time. In the morning, she would check back with Jasmin to learn if the Florida police had managed to track down Cathy Zimmer.

"There's nothing more for any of us to do here tonight," Peyton said. "Do you need a place to stay?"

Willow exchanged a glance with Theo. She supposed they could take the chopper back, but it was late, and the noise would disturb the lodge's guests. She didn't really want to drive. It had been a long day, and she was tired, physically and emotionally. "We do."

"You both can stay here," Peyton said. "Theo, I'm sure Jonathan wouldn't mind you taking his cot. Willow, you can stay at my place."

That sounded like the perfect solution—and the best way to gain a little distance from her husband. "Thank you."

As morning neared, Theo repositioned himself on the cot in the small bunk room of the

PNK9 training center, staring at the ceiling. He'd slept little through the night as his mind replayed his conversation with Willow.

It's not weakness to ask for help.

Did she believe he was concerned with how it might make him look to seek help? It hurt to think she would consider him so prideful. It wasn't that he thought it would make him look weak but was more that he didn't feel he deserved help from anyone. He could barely allow her, the woman whom he'd pledged to honor and cherish, to see his rotted core.

Yet he wanted to be worthy of Willow. Worthy of her love once again. Would requesting professional assistance give him back the life he and Willow had once shared?

Noises from inside the training center cut off his thoughts. There was no mistaking Willow's voice. He rose, put on his shoes and left the bunk room to find Willow and Star.

They were with Peyton and another woman who held the leash to a brown and white beagle.

Theo had eyes only for his wife. She looked refreshed and pretty. His heart ached with longing. She'd changed from the summery dress of the night before into a clean uniform. The green color made her blue eyes sparkle.

"Sleep well?" she asked.

He shrugged, unwilling to admit how consumed his thoughts had been of her and their future.

"Theo, this is Layla Miller," Willow introduced the green-eyed, blonde woman. "She's been with the unit for three months."

"Nice to meet you," Theo said, tearing his attention away from Willow. Layla was petite but strong-looking.

Layla gestured to the cute beagle at her side. "And this little lady is Bixby."

"I'm working with Bixby," Peyton said. "She's being cross-trained in narcotics and weapon detection."

Theo chuckled. "She's very unassuming. No one will realize she's on the job."

Layla grinned. "Yep. That's what we're counting on."

"Donovan is giving us a new SUV to use," Willow told him. "He's having the other one towed in for repairs."

"Great. Any word on Jonathan?" Theo asked.

"He's stable," Peyton offered. "I'm going to go visit him later today."

"There's been no word on the puppies," Willow said.

Not what he wanted to hear. "I'll check in with my boss," he promised. "Have you eaten?"

"No, I was waiting for you," Willow said with a gentle smile.

He loved that smile. "We can stop on the way out of town."

With a nod, Willow hugged Peyton goodbye. "Keep me updated on Jonathan and the puppies."

"You do the same," Peyton said with a meaningful look toward Theo.

He wondered if Willow had confided in her about their marital problems and their impending parenthood. And what exactly she'd told her.

Back at the Stark Lodge, after a shower and a change of clothes, Theo knocked on the door connecting their rooms.

When Willow opened the door, apparently ready for the day, he grinned. "Want to go for a walk?"

Her hair was braided, and she carried her backpack. "You read my mind."

"Not sure about that, but I do know you, and I figured you'd probably want to go out." He nodded his chin to Star, who wore her ballistics vest. "And Star would want to stretch her legs."

"I think we could all use some time outside after the drive," Willow said. "Parker and Brandie will meet us at the trail."

"Perfect." He locked his room door, then walked out through Willow's hotel room, making sure the door locked behind them. When they reached the trailhead behind the Stark Lodge, they found Parker and Brandie talking with two park rangers, the woman and the shorter of the two men they'd met a few days ago.

Theo's gaze snagged on the patch ironed onto the sleeve of the forest rangers' shirts. Something about the icon niggled at the back of his mind, though why he couldn't say. He'd seen it numerous times over the years.

"We were wondering if there was any more news on the bomber?" Ranger Kathleen said to Willow.

"Nothing concrete," Willow said. "Have you ever heard of a man named Charles Zimmer?"

The two park rangers shook their heads.

"Doesn't sound familiar," Ranger Mitch said. "Who is he?"

"A person of interest," Theo stated. "Have there been any more incidents in the past twenty-four hours?"

"None," Kathleen said. "We hope that means the bomber has decided to stop. Our boss is very concerned by the publicity. Our number of visitors per day has dropped dramatically since the first bombing, and reservations have declined."

"Not surprising," Parker said. "Civilians don't go where they don't feel safe."

"We pride ourselves on making our parks safe." Kathleen's defensiveness rang loud and clear.

"Of course you do." Willow shot Parker a censuring glare. "We are all trying to make the parks safe."

"We stopped in to tell you a construction team will cut up the tree that was felled," Mitch said. "Our boss thought you should know."

"Thank you for the information," Willow said. "You have my number. Keep us informed if you see anything suspicious."

Theo tracked the two rangers as they walked back to their utility vehicle. A sticker on the back window matching the icon on the rangers' shirts jogged his memory.

"Hold up." He hurried to catch up with them, aware of Willow and Star close on his heels, followed by the two recruits.

Pointing to the sticker, Theo asked, "Do all the park rangers have that sticker in the back window of their vehicles?"

"Yes," came Mitch's response. "Even our personal ones."

"Any chance you know someone who owns a silver 4x4 pickup truck with that sticker on the back window?"

The two forest rangers exchanged a glance.

"Our boss, Ranger Steve Adkins, has a silver 4x4," Kathleen said.

Willow let out a slight gasp and met his gaze. "You don't think...?"

"I'm not sure what to think," Theo quickly cut her off. "But we need to go talk to Ranger Steve."

Mitch's dark eyes widened with concern. "Is there an issue we should be concerned with?"

Not wanting to cast aspersions on Ranger Steve without proof that he had been the person driving the pickup truck that tried to make them crash, Theo said, "I hope not, but we'll let you know."

THIRTEEN

Willow waited until the two park rangers had pulled out of the parking lot of the Stark Lodge before she gave in to the question burning in her mind. "If Ranger Steve Adkins is the person who hit our SUV, then does that make him the bomber, as well?"

"We won't know until we talk with him," Theo answered. "Though he doesn't fit the profile. But profiling isn't an exact science."

"He was so helpful that day we met him in the ranger station, and Star didn't alert on him."

"His helpfulness could have been a smoke screen."

She didn't want to be cynical, but Theo was right. Ranger Steve had been studying the map when they'd walked into the station. Was it because he was plotting his next explosion rather than trying to figure out the bomber's motive? How did Charles Zimmer fit into the picture?

"Ranger Steve Adkins and Charles Zimmer could be working together. Maybe Steve is the one in charge, he decides where to place the devices and Charles sets the explosives."

"Who's Charles Zimmer?" Parker asked.

"A person of interest." Theo brought up the DMV photo of Charles on his phone and showed both of the candidates. "This is an old photo. He may look different now."

"His fingerprint was found on the blasting cap discovered near the felled tree that nearly crushed us," Willow told Parker and Brandie. She decided not to fill them in on her history with Charles. They didn't need to know every little detail.

Theo arched his eyebrows but didn't comment. She gave him a slight shrug. He might not always know her reasons, but he was doing a better job of accepting her decisions. A suspiciously familiar warmth spread through her chest.

"Is Steve the guy we met at the ranger station near where you were hurt?" Brandie asked.

Willow suppressed a shudder at the reminder of how close she'd been to the explosion. "Yes, Ranger Steve is the one who informed us about the proposed all-terrain vehicle trail cutting through the park."

"If his goal is to stay under the radar and

blow stuff up, it seems odd he'd tell you about the new trail, where you'd be sure to patrol," Parker reasoned.

Seeing his logic, she nodded. "It does indeed."

If she hadn't had the map Steve had given to her marked with the new all-terrain vehicle trail, she never would have headed in the direction of the proposed entrance. And wouldn't have been in the path of the tree. How had the bomber known she was there? She'd had the creepy sensation of someone observing her. A twig had snapped. Clearly, the bomber had been watching her. Stalking her. But who was the bomber? Steve or Charles? Was there a third person involved? Or had Steve given her that map to set her up to be killed? Why?

"Theo and I will visit Steve," Willow told Parker and Brandie. "I'd like you both to provide protection for the tree removal crew. There's no telling whether or not one of our suspects might try to sabotage their efforts."

Brandie's eyes widened. "You trust us with this?"

Willow hoped and prayed nothing would happen, but she couldn't be in two places at once. And she wasn't going to send rookies to Steve in case what they suspected was true. How would he react when they approached him?

She couldn't have anything happen to the candidates on her watch. Empathy for the pain Theo had suffered after the loss of his informant tightened her chest. "I do trust you. Just make sure no one messes with the tree removal crew. Call in if you see anything suspicious. And I mean anything. A person watching who shouldn't be there…any strange equipment that doesn't belong to the crew…anything that doesn't feel right to you."

Parker and Brandie, with their dogs, hustled over to their SUV, bickering over who would drive. They seemed so young to her, even though they were both trained K-9 officers.

Shaking her head, Willow remembered her first days in law enforcement. Remembered the giddy and nerve-racking sensation of being responsible for the welfare of others. Even now, she had that same sort of tension lodged like a fist in her gut. She could only imagine how much anguish Theo had been tormented with over the past year. She resisted the need to comfort him. Now was not the time. But soon. Until then, she had to stay on task.

She turned to Theo. "I'd better call Donovan to fill him in on this new development. I'll have Jasmin run a background check on Park Ranger Steve Adkins."

Theo nodded. "And I'll have his name run

through the FBI database as well. But I have to admit, I'm not liking him as the bomber."

Not surprised Theo would want to use his own resources, Willow gave him a thumbs-up. She also had doubts that Steve was the person terrorizing the park. "The more information we can gather, the better armed we will be."

"True." He winked and moved away to make his call.

Watching him, a flood of tender emotions filled her to overflowing. But she had to contain them and set them aside so she could call Donovan and let him know what they had just learned. "We've been told that Ranger Steve Adkins has a truck matching the description of the one that came after us."

"Go have a chat with Adkins. Be careful," Donovan said. "Keep me informed. Let me know if I need to send more backup your way."

"We're not expecting trouble from Ranger Steve. He's the one who pointed out the possible motive of the bomber. I think if he were the one setting off the charges, he wouldn't be so careless as to direct us to where he was placing them. I sent the two candidates shadowing us to monitor the removal of the felled tree," she told him. "In case there's an issue there."

"Good thinking. I'll touch base with Parker

and Brandie," Donovan said. "It says a lot that you feel comfortable sending them off alone."

"They're both capable," she told him. "I like them. I think either one will add a lot to our unit."

"I'll keep that in mind," Donovan said before disconnecting.

Willow pocketed her phone as Theo walked over with the keys to the SUV in hand. "My guy's looking into Ranger Steve. You can make the rest of your calls on the road."

Hopping into the passenger seat of the SUV, Willow itched to get answers from Steve.

As Theo drove, she called Jasmin.

"I was just going to call you," Jasmin said by way of answering the phone. "I have news about Cathy Zimmer."

Putting the call on her phone's speaker, Willow said, "I'm here with Theo. I have you on speaker. Tell us what you discovered."

"Cathy Zimmer lives in a retirement community in Boca Raton, Florida. Five days ago, Cathy left on a Mediterranean cruise with a group from the community. One of her neighbors is watching her cat and watering her plants."

"Has the neighbor seen Charles?" Theo asked.

"Not in over a year," Jasmin informed them.

"Her neighbor says Cathy is a fun person to be around. She's always organizing activities like the cruise."

"Is there any way to reach her on the ship?" Theo asked.

"Possibly. I'll reach out," Jasmin said. "Anything else?"

"I have another quick search for you to do," Willow said. "Find everything you can on Steve Adkins. He's a park ranger with the forest service stationed in the Olympic National Park."

"Will do," Jasmin promised. "Is he somehow connected to Charles Zimmer?"

"At this point we don't know," Willow replied. "But he owns a silver pickup truck like the one that tried to crash into us yesterday. I'd like to have a little information before we talk to him. We're on our way there now."

"I'll get right on it." Jasmin clicked off.

"Sounds like Charles and his mother aren't too close," Theo stated. "That could mean any number of things. And she does live on the other side of the country."

"For her sake, I hope she doesn't know what her son is up to," Willow said and dialed Peyton's cell phone number.

When her friend answered, Willow said,

"Hey, it's Willow. Just checking to see if there's an update on Jonathan and the puppies."

"No news on the puppies," Peyton said. "I'm worried about them. I hope whoever has them is feeding them properly and giving them plenty of water. This time away from their training isn't good. When we find them, I will have to do some retraining."

"That's too bad." Willow sent up a quick prayer for the puppies' safety. "And Jonathan?"

"He came around this morning," Peyton said. "He can't identify who came up behind him and hit him. All he remembers is the puppies growling and someone clocking him on the head."

"We don't have cameras in that play yard, do we?"

"We don't. But Donovan has ordered them. They'll be installed ASAP."

"Good. I'm here for you if you need anything," Willow said.

"Back at you."

The phone beeped with another incoming call—from Jasmin. Willow ended the call with Peyton and answered. "Jasmin?"

"Hey, so I did some digging on Steve Adkins, and there are no red flags. He's married, two kids. Pays his taxes and doesn't have any outstanding warrants. Not even a parking ticket."

"Great," Willow said. "I appreciate you being so quick."

Willow slipped her phone back into her pocket as Theo turned onto the fire road and followed it to the ranger station but parked out of sight of the building.

Theo and Willow cautiously climbed out of the vehicle, closing their doors softly to not alert anyone to their presence. After releasing Star from her compartment, Willow and Theo approached the ranger station. Nearby, beneath the shade of a tree, was a silver 4x4 truck. The license plate had been smeared with mud, and in the corner of the rear window was a National Park Service sticker, matching the one on the park rangers' shirts.

Theo gestured to the truck, indicating they should go around front of the vehicle to be sure it was indeed the same truck. The damaged front bumper and grille left them with no doubt.

The question was, who had been driving? Charles Zimmer?

Or was Steve involved?

Confusion tightened the muscles along Willow's shoulders.

"I'm going to text for backup," she whispered.

Theo gave her a thumbs-up sign.

Fingers flying over the small keyboard on her phone, Willow sent a note to Donovan explaining about the truck, then sent a text to Brandie and Parker, giving them their location. The two candidates would come right away.

At the entrance of the ranger station, they could hear two men in a heated argument. One of the voices Willow recognized as Ranger Steve Adkins's. He sounded distressed. Was he in trouble?

They needed to get inside and assess the situation.

Theo placed his hand on his holstered weapon and eased the door open. At his nod, Willow and Star stepped inside and followed the sound of angry voices to the small back office, where they stopped in the doorway.

"You owe me," a gravelly voice insisted.

"You'll cover whatever damages insurance doesn't," Steve Adkins said to the other man.

Steve, dressed in his uniform of gray shirt and green trousers, stood behind a desk, red-faced and angry. Across from him stood a bearded man, wearing the same uniform but topped with a jacket as well as a flat-brimmed hat covering his shaved head. Willow recognized Chaz Jones from the cleanup crew after the second trailhead marker bombing. He had his hands on the desk. Both men's gazes turned to Willow, Theo and Star.

Chaz abruptly straightened and shoved his hands into his jacket pockets.

Star pulled at her leash. Willow allowed the dog to do her job, giving her slack on her leash. She headed straight for Chaz, sniffing at his boots and pant legs. Then she barked and sat, staring at him. She was alerting, just as she had at the trail marker.

Chaz stepped away with a scowl.

Steve's expression turned to surprise and confusion. "Officer Bates. Special Agent Bates. You're back. What can I do for you?"

"Is that your silver truck outside?" Theo asked.

"It is," Steve said warily, with a glance to Chaz. "Is there a problem?"

"Yes, as a matter of fact, there is." Theo stated. "Were you driving that vehicle yesterday afternoon?"

"No." Steve's lips pressed together, and he glared at Chaz. "Why do you ask?"

"Someone used that vehicle to ram into our SUV, trying to cause us to crash on Highway 101 as we were returning from Forks," Theo said.

Willow stepped closer to Chaz, searching his face. His beard was thick and dark.

He wore no glasses, but there was something about him that resembled the old DMV photo of Charles Zimmer. Going out on a limb, she said, "Chaz. Short for Charles?"

Chaz's gaze narrowed, and he stepped farther away but didn't say anything.

Star followed him and sat again, using her passive alert. Chaz, aka Charles Zimmer, had explosive residue on him. Was there another device set to explode in the park? Was Charles even a real ranger? Or just dressed like one? Was Steve covering for him?

Her gaze bounced between Steve and Charles. What were these two planning?

Theo could barely contain his anger. One of these two men had used that silver pickup truck to try to hurt him and Willow and their baby. Was that what the two men were arguing over? Were they working together?

And Star was alerting on Charles Zimmer.

Needing clarity, Theo said to Steve, "If you weren't driving the truck yesterday afternoon, who was?"

Steve folded his arms over his chest and glared at Charles. "What did you do? You said a deer ran out in front of you. Why would you ram my truck into their vehicle?"

"I didn't. They have no proof of anything," Charles said, continuing to back toward the exit.

Willow advanced on him as she reeled in Star's leash. "There's nowhere for you to go, Charles."

"Charles Zimmer, you're under arrest." Theo removed zip ties from his pocket and headed toward the ranger. "Put your hands up and turn around."

Star barked as if to punctuate Theo's instructions.

"Keep that dog away from me," Charles demanded, stepping menacingly toward Willow.

Apprehension bolted down Theo's spine. "Willow!"

Before Willow had time to move, Charles grabbed her by the arm, yanking her to him at the same time he pulled a KA-BAR knife from the pocket of his jacket and held the shiny blade to her neck.

Drawing his weapon, Theo's stomach dropped. He couldn't let this man hurt her.

"Chaz, what are you doing?" Steve yelled. "Put that knife away. This isn't how a ranger behaves."

Flicking Steve a dismissive glare, Charles said, "Step back, agent man. If you don't, I make her bleed."

Theo met Willow's gaze. He could see the

sparks of anger in her blue eyes. Keeping his weapon trained on Charles's head, Theo said, "There's nowhere for you to go. More officers are on the way. Surrender now and things will go easy on you."

Charles shuffled to the side, keeping Willow in front of him and the knife pressed to her tender skin. "Move over there, by the desk."

Theo stood his ground. "Drop the weapon."

Charles pressed the knife harder against Willow's skin. Blood beaded and slowly dripped down the blade.

Horror slammed into Theo. He couldn't let this happen. He couldn't let Willow get hurt. A wave of rage crashed over him. But he didn't dare take the shot, for fear Charles would sink the blade deeper into Willow's neck.

Agitated, Star barked and growled.

Charles kicked at Star.

Willow released her hold on the leash, allowing the dog to dance away out of Charles's reach. And she used Charles's distraction to elbow him in the gut. Theo wanted to cheer as Charles took the blow with a curse, the knife slipping from his hand.

Theo lunged forward, preparing to tackle Charles, but the distance was too wide and Charles recovered too quickly.

Charles released his hold on Willow's arm

and grabbed her weapon from her holster and placed it against her head. "I'm in charge here. You understand!"

Willow stilled, her eyes going wide.

"Yes," Theo placated as fear ramped up the adrenaline in his veins. "We understand."

Charles yanked on Willow's arm and shoved her forward. "You and me are leaving, unless you want to be dead now." Charles rammed the barrel of the weapon into Willow's ribs. "Any more funny business like that elbow shot and I won't hesitate to kill you."

Theo had to keep Willow safe. He lifted his hands. "Take me. Let her go."

Charles snorted. "Put your gun and your cell phone on the desk."

Complying grated on Theo's nerves, but he couldn't let Charles hurt Willow and their baby.

"Pick up the knife," Charles ordered Willow. "And don't try anything or I'll shoot you."

Willow bent to retrieve the knife. Star moved to her side and licked her face.

"Hurry up," Charles demanded.

Willow touched Star as if to reassure her before she rose. Charles grabbed the knife from her hand and tucked it back into his jacket pocket.

Latching onto Willow's arm and jamming

the gun into her ribs again, he said, "We're walking out of here, nice and easy. The dog and the agent are staying behind." He looked at Steve. "By the way, I quit."

"Chaz, you don't want to do this," Steve implored.

"Of course I do," Charles said. "This was always how it was going to end."

He pushed Willow toward the door.

Theo had to fight every instinct not to launch himself at Charles. He could see the man's finger was on the trigger. There were two lives at stake here. He couldn't lose either one.

Theo followed Charles and Willow out of the ranger station. Charles pushed Willow to the silver truck. Then Charles swung the gun and fired at the PNK9 Unit SUV, taking out the right front tire. The sound echoed through the trees and assaulted Theo's ears. Willow winced.

Frantically barking, Star rushed toward Charles. The gun swung to Star.

Willow screamed, "No, Star!" She tried to break free from Charles's grip, but the man held on to her.

Theo stepped on Star's leash, drawing the dog up short.

"Bravo, agent man," Charles said. Then he pushed Willow into the driver seat, making her scoot over into the passenger seat while he climbed in behind her. Within seconds the silver 4x4 pickup truck was roaring down the fire road in a spray of gravel.

Theo let out a howl of rage. Then he ran to the SUV.

Steve ran out of the building with Theo's weapon and cell phone.

Taking them from the ranger, Theo barked out, "Call 911. Report your truck stolen. Tell them the Olympic National Forest serial bomber is driving and he's kidnapped Officer Willow Bates."

As Steve made the call, Theo went to work on changing the tire. The lug nuts were hard to turn, and Theo took all his frustration out on them. He managed to get the spare tire in place. It would work for a while. Theo jumped into the driver's seat. With Star strapped in next to him on the front passenger seat, Theo tore down the fire road, praying he could find Willow before it was too late.

Driving as fast as he dared on the spare tire, Theo hit the main highway and slammed to a stop. He didn't know which direction to go. He had to rescue Willow, to make sure she and their child lived. He needed to tell her he loved her and would do whatever was necessary, even counseling, if that's what it took, to win back her heart.

Futile rage had him banging his fists on the steering wheel. Reining in helpless frustration, he dialed Donovan.

"Fanelli," Donovan's voice filled the cab of the SUV.

"I need your help," Theo said. "Charles Zimmer just kidnapped Willow. He has been going by the name of Chaz Jones and working as a park ranger. And he's the one who tried to cause our accident yesterday. I don't know where he's taken her or which direction they've gone."

Theo could hear the panic roaring in his voice, and he tried to hang on to his composure. He couldn't lose her. He just couldn't.

FOURTEEN

Willow grabbed the truck door handle as Charles hung another sharp right turn, taking them onto a barely visible dirt road cut through the forest. Sunlight flashed through the branches like a strobe, causing her to blink rapidly. Huge ferns slapped against the sides of the truck. Twisting, spindly branches of vine maples hit the windows like cracking whips. They'd been traveling for twenty minutes before he'd taken a side road and then another and another. He obviously was well versed in how to get around the park.

"Where are we going?" she asked. "Why are you doing this?"

He remained silent, his concentration on driving.

Trying again, she pushed, "You know you'll never get away with kidnapping me. People will be looking for me. My husband will track you down. He's with the FBI. There's nowhere you'll be able to run."

"Shut up!"

The pickup truck bumped along the old service road with jarring impacts as the tires bounced over potholes and protruding roots. He was taking them deep into the middle of the park. Was his intent to shoot her and leave her body in the woods?

Sharp, ugly fear spread through her limbs like splintered wood, but she would not give in to the terror. She would survive. For herself, for Theo and their child.

She didn't know how long it would take Theo to change the tire on the disabled SUV. Even if he was able to replace the bullet-punctured tire with the spare, there was no way for him to know which direction they'd gone on the main road, let alone all the seemingly random turns on the dirt roads. There was no way he would be able to find her.

Not unless she could turn on her GPS tracker. But the way Charles was driving, she didn't dare let go of the door handle for fear she'd go flying across the seat. He might actually shoot her accidentally. Before he had a chance to shoot her purposefully? No. She had to find a way out of this mess.

"How long have you worked for the forestry

service?" She assessed him, comparing him to how he looked in his DMV photo. He'd lost weight and gained muscles while working in the forest service. He'd ditched the glasses for contacts and shaved his head but let his beard fill in, full and bushy. "Why did you change your name?"

He flicked her a glance and pressed his lips tight.

Apparently, she wasn't going to get answers.

Finally, they ran out of road, the forest forming an impenetrable wall of greenery in front of them, and Charles slammed on the brakes so hard the truck slid to a jarring stop. Willow pitched forward, barely managing to brace herself to keep from hitting her forehead on the dashboard.

Charles shoved the gun in her face. "Get out!"

She scrambled out the passenger door. He slid across the seat and followed her. Then he placed his hand on her back to shove her forward. "Move it."

Stumbling but able to catch her balance, she asked, "Where are we going?"

"You'll see." He directed her toward a defined hiking trail, but she had no idea which one it was without the benefit of a map or trail marker. He was right beside her, the gun once again pressed to her side.

The same side as her GPS tracker. If she reached for the tracker in the small leather pouch on her utility belt, to turn on the two-inch-square device, he'd notice and think she was reaching for the gun and shoot. She needed a distraction.

Scanning the moss-covered trees, tall lacy ferns and thick brush, she looked for signs of other humans, but they were so deep in the woods, off the marked trails, she doubted there were many hikers who made it this far.

She tried again to engage him. "Are you close with your mother? Did you know she was on a cruise?"

"Don't talk to me," he grumbled.

Setting her gaze to the path, she noticed a protruding root up ahead, barely visible amid the dirt and carpet of moss growing over the ground. Willow readied her limbs as she drew closer to the root, preparing herself for a fall. Sending a prayer that her idea would work, she pretended to catch her foot on the root, going down on her hands and knees. Charles had no choice but to release his hold on her or go down with her.

"Hey!" he yelled.

She took advantage of the moment to flip on

the GPS beacon. Knowing Theo would have already alerted the K-9 unit of her kidnapping, she was confident that when the beacon activated at headquarters, they would know where to find her. And inform her husband. He would find her. Hope flared bright within her, warming her heart and her mind.

She would survive this. For her baby, and for Theo.

"Get up!" Charles yanked on her hair.

Pain ricocheted through her skull. "Okay, okay." She stood, bracing her feet apart to keep from toppling over for real as a wave of dizziness washed over her. "I tripped. Give me a break."

"No," he snapped. "Why should I? No one has ever given *me* a break. Why should I give you one?"

Dusting the dirt from her hands on her pant legs and hoping for a moment to catch her breath, she said, "You've had a good life. Didn't you like being a park ranger?"

"What is with all the questions?" He huffed. But as if he couldn't help himself when it came to talking about the forest, he said, "Of course I like being a park ranger. I love it. I love protecting the park. That's what I'm doing."

Did he really believe what he was doing was good for the forest? "How do you figure?"

He made a scoffing noise. "Stop talking and start moving!"

Charles kept them hiking, cutting a trail through the dense foliage at a grueling pace. Willow tried to keep her bearings, but Charles had them zigzagging through the forest, dipping off the carved paths and bushwhacking through the ferns and sprawling vine maple trees, then returning to what trail there was. It looked to be more of a game trail than anything else. They'd long since deviated away from the main hiking trail, where they might have encountered others.

"Did you bring water? Protein bars?" she asked. "Anything?"

He huffed out an aggrieved breath. "You're fine. Keep moving."

She took that as a sign the answer was no. He hadn't packed for this hike, which meant coming out here was impulsive. He could have gone anywhere with her as his captive. Why the forest? What was he planning?

They traversed deeper and deeper into the woods. The light slanting more steeply through the tree canopy was her only indication of the passage of time. She wished for her phone, if only to check the time, but more to call for help. She had to stay hopeful that her team would find her before Charles did anything permanent—like kill her.

The dense, moss-laden trees formed a sort of cocoon around them as they moved. Verdant green leaves danced on limbs as they brushed past. Little noise penetrated through the forest. Her muscles burned as the incline of the terrain increased. The air grew thin and colder. She had a sinking feeling they were climbing toward Blue Glacier. A place she and Theo had visited on several occasions in the early days of their marriage. The spectacular view from the top of the glacier drew hikers from around the world.

However, to get to the top of the glacier, they would first have to navigate the decades-old washout left by a past storm, which would require them to use a ladder down into the wash and then climb back up on the other side. A taxing trip in the best of circumstances.

Her throat itched. A headache formed behind her eyes. Dehydration setting in? "Why are we going to Blue Glacier?"

"Figured out where we are, did you?" He chuckled, but there was no humor behind the noise.

She steadied her breath, trying to keep her senses alert so she could survive this ordeal. Dizziness threatened to take her to the ground.

She managed to keep from staggering as she continued forward. There was still so much to do in life. She regretted not telling Theo that she loved him unconditionally. Because she realized she did. She had had no right to put conditions on their relationship. To expect him to bare his secrets because she'd asked and wouldn't have understood the pain he was going through. Then, when he did open up, she'd demanded he seek help from someone else. Though she still believed she wasn't qualified to guide him to healing, she could listen without judgment. She could love him through the hard parts. Wasn't that part of the vows she took at their wedding? She sent up a prayer for forgiveness. And prayers for protection for herself, for the baby and for Theo.

"Hurry up. Stop lagging," Charles groused.

She tried to pick up the pace, but her legs trembled from the exertion. She needed to slow him down, to distract him again by getting him talking. "Why are you doing this, Charles?"

"Because you forced my hand. If you'd heeded my warnings to stay out of my way, you wouldn't be here now." He shook his head. "I knew you were trouble when I saw you and the dog at the trailhead. Even though I didn't know who you were at first."

Reliving that moment on the trail moments

before the marker exploded, she shuddered and slowed her steps. "So, you are the person who pushed me."

"Yes." His tone suggested she was an imbecile. "Obviously, I didn't push you hard enough, or you would've been closer to the blast and out of my hair."

Apparently, he noticed she'd slowed, because he nudged her forward, his hand on her back, inches from where the stitches in her shoulder still pulled.

Only picking up her pace by a half measure, she asked, "When did you figure out who I was?"

"Later, when you introduced yourself when we were cleaning up. I put it together. How many Willows could there possibly be?"

She swallowed the outrage and sorrow floating to the surface. "You know my dad was the man killed with your father?"

"I do," Charles ground out with a hostility she didn't understand. Was his anger directed at her or the person who killed their fathers? Or both?

"You're angry. I'm angry, too."

Charles snorted. "And just like your dad, you were somewhere you shouldn't have been. Wrong place, wrong time."

"I was doing my job." Though her mind

stuck on his reference to her dad. What was that about? "You are the one hurting the park."

"No, I'm protecting the forest," he insisted.

"By blowing up trail markers and bringing down healthy trees?" She didn't mention trying to kill her and Theo. The last thing she needed was to agitate him more.

"I can't let them put in that trail," he said. "It will ruin everything."

"I don't disagree with you," she said. "But this isn't the way."

"You sound like my mother," he grumbled. "She is always saying there are better ways to make improvements. But no one listens unless you *make* them listen."

Thinking of his mother, she asked, "Why go by Chaz Jones?"

"Do you know what it was like being a Zimmer after my father was killed?" he said. "The pity. I got sick of it and took on my mother's maiden name and used the nickname my high school wrestling coach gave me."

"My father was killed that same day. I experienced the pity, too."

He snorted. "Nobody was supposed to die. You and your father interfered. Just like you're trying to interfere now."

Horror spread through her, causing her to misstep and stumble. "What does that mean?"

His words sent havoc through her system. "How do you know no one was supposed to die?"

"Don't you get it?" He stopped and stared at her. His eyes were hard. "My pops and me set that bomb. We didn't like that they put in a new entrance to the national park and were taking people's money. The park should be free and for everyone to enjoy."

Her mind reeled. She couldn't have heard him right. She reached out to steady herself, but there was nothing to hold on to. "You and your father set that explosive?"

"My dad tried to stop your dad from getting too close," Charles said. "But your dad wouldn't listen. Just like you wouldn't listen."

A tight fist of rage squeezed the breath from her lungs. The tragedy of her father's death had shaped her life from that point forward. "You and your father killed my father."

He slashed the air with the gun. "No, *you* killed them."

Her confusion must have shown on her face.

Waving the gun at her, he yelled, "I was there, at your father's funeral. I heard you say if you hadn't wanted to go hiking that day, he'd be alive."

His words taunted her, stirring up her guilt and shame. The millions of recriminations she'd heaped upon herself every day since the disaster that had robbed her of her father.

"If you hadn't insisted on going out hiking, then you wouldn't have been there," Charles screamed, his voice absorbed by the moss-laden trees. "And my father would be alive!"

Despite the anguish she'd carried for so long, she shot back with defensive anger, "It could just as easily have been some other person who had gone up to the kiosk at that moment." She wanted to claw his eyes out. "Why would you plant a bomb in the middle of the morning, when you know people would be coming and going, if you didn't intend for someone to die?"

His mouth pressed into a thin line beneath his beard. "It was the only time we could get near the kiosk without anybody being suspicious." He gave her a hard shove. "Keep moving."

Willow took a step, then another, desperately fighting the urge to be sick.

Theo drove, searching for the silver truck driven by the man who'd stolen his wife. How far had Charles and Willow traveled? What if they'd turned off on one of the many country roads? What if Theo was headed in the wrong direction?

Donovan said he would send the chopper to

search from the air, but with all the tree coverage, Donovan wasn't hopeful the truck would be spotted.

His phone rang, and he hit the Bluetooth button on the center of the steering wheel.

"Bates."

Donovan's voice filled the SUV. "Willow turned on her GPS beacon, and an alert was sent to the department. I'm patching you in to Jasmin now. She'll give you directions. I'm on my way in the chopper. I'm sending everyone available to the location."

Theo could hardly breathe. "Thanks, Chief," he managed to choke out.

"Don't worry, Theo. We'll find them."

Them. Willow and his child. The loves of his life. *Please, Lord, please, don't let anything bad happen to them.*

Jasmin's voice came on the line. Her soothing tone helped to calm his nerves as he listened to the directions she doled out like nuggets of candy. He cherished each piece as he moved closer to finding Willow.

He missed a turn the first time and had to double back, but he finally found the barely there road off the main highway, then a series of turns that drew him deeper into the forest. Star whined as the SUV bumped and rattled along the rutted and pitted road until it was hardly even passable. He'd lost cell service a while back, but not before Jasmin assured him Willow's beacon was moving toward Blue Glacier. Which meant she was alive. But for how much longer?

He swallowed down the surge of bile. No. He wouldn't go there. Not yet.

Moss hung off the large, thick-limbed trees and created a closed-in effect that had his heart rate skyrocketing. Where would this joke of a road lead? Would he find Willow?

Up ahead, the silver pickup truck loomed. Theo brought the SUV to a halt as his heart froze in his chest. He withdrew his weapon and grabbed Star's leash. Theo climbed out of the vehicle, and Star jumped out after him. Approaching the truck cautiously, Theo held his breath, praying he wouldn't find Willow's dead body inside.

The truck was empty. He breathed out a measure of relief. But where had they gone? There was an overgrown but distinct trail up ahead. He studied the ground, seeing footprints in the dirt where there was no vegetation growing.

To Star, Theo said, "Find Willow."

Star's nose twitched, then she put her snout to the ground and started hustling along the path. Theo prayed they got to Willow in time.

* * *

Blue Glacier loomed up ahead in the distance. Sunlight glinted off the ice shards dotting the landscape. The trees had thinned as they neared the meadow leading to the washout, where the ground dropped steeply away. A ladder lay on the slope, and a separate rope attached to a tree provided the only real means of descending into the wash. Then they'd have to make the arduous climb up the other side to reach the glacier.

Willow shivered, wrapping her arms around her middle. She wasn't dressed for this climate. But she knew how to survive in the wilderness. She just needed to get Charles to drop his guard long enough so she could disarm him.

Or for Theo to find her. As much as she wanted to believe he would stop at nothing to rescue her, she had to save herself. She had to save her child.

"Charles, I need you to understand, I'm on your side. I don't want the all-terrain vehicle trail to go through the park any more than you do."

"Right. Then why are you trying to stop me from destroying their route?"

"Because that's not the way to make the change you want," she told him. "The Pacific Northwest K9 unit has resources," she told him. "We know a very rich philanthropist who I believe would lobby against the route. All we need to do is approach him. You and I, together, we could do that. For our fathers."

"I'm doing this for our fathers. For my father. He wanted the park to be free to everyone. He wanted to keep the forest from becoming a tourist trap."

They stopped at the edge of the washout. The ground had been disturbed. Apprehension recoiled through Willow. "Charles, what did you do here?"

"Did you know they want the ATVs to come up the wash?" He gestured to the bottom of the steep ravine. "They intend to ride all the way up. I can't let that happen."

Dreading what his solution to the problem might be, she said, "How do you intend to stop it?"

"I'm going to make it so that no one can ever pass through here except on foot or horseback. I'm going to cave in the washout."

"You planted explosives along the ridge?" The horror of what he wanted to do clawed through her, making her pulse pound in her ears.

"It's what I do."

The pride in his tone set her teeth on edge. "But you'll kill us both."

"I'm ready to die for the cause. Are you?"

No! she silently screamed. She wanted to live. She wanted to raise her child with her husband. With Theo.

Fearing she'd never get to see Theo again because any rescue attempts would be too late, she only had one move left.

She had to disarm Charles before he detonated the explosives. Once he triggered the bomb—or, more likely, *bombs*—the whole ridge would collapse, taking them down with tons of earth and house-size boulders. And who knew if the explosions would trigger an avalanche on the glacier? Depending on the number and strength of explosives he'd planted, the detonation could have a ripple effect throughout the whole park.

She readied her body to strike, praying for an opportunity.

Charles bent to pick something up off the ground, and she struck. Hitting him in the face with her elbow, then stomping down hard on his instep.

The gun flew from his hand. Willow lunged for it.

But he was quicker than she anticipated.

He grabbed her arm and swung her around to face him. She barely had time to blink before he rammed his forehead into hers, connecting so hard she saw lights pop behind her eyes. Pain exploded through her head as her teeth slammed together. She stumbled backward, nearly slipping over the edge. He yanked her forward and threw her to the ground.

He pounced, straddling her with the KA-BAR knife to her throat. "Don't you want to wait and see the fireworks?"

FIFTEEN

Moss-draped branches hanging low like greedy fingers trying to snatch away all hope kept Theo on edge as he and Star worked their way through the thick, dense forest. The trail they followed was barely passable. Ruts and roots made the way treacherous. Star pulled at the leash, wanting to go off the trail. Had Willow and Charles deviated from this path?

Anxiety twisted through Theo's gut. Would he find Willow? Would it be too late when he did?

What was Charles's endgame? Why kidnap Willow? If his intent was to get away and not face justice for his crimes, why had Charles taken her deep into the forest?

Star stopped in her tracks and pulled hard to the right.

"Really?" Theo peered into the murky woods filled with dark shadows and eerie vegetation that brought to mind the unnerving Mirkwood Forest of Tolkien's *Lord of the Rings*. Willow loved those books and movies. He enjoyed them because she did.

Only Theo hoped there weren't giant spiders crawling along the limbs of the trees or waiting to pounce behind a hollowed-out remnant of an old cedar.

Suppressing a shudder and motivated by the thought that Willow could be trapped somewhere in the overgrown timberland, there was only one thing Theo could do—he had to trust Star to find Willow.

And that meant going off any marked trail, no matter how unappealing the idea. For him, hunting prey usually involved a concrete jungle, fast car chases and entering buildings with his weapon ready. Climbing over dead logs, careful not to trip on protruding roots, fighting through abundant ferns and avoiding the clinging vines proved to require a good deal of concentration. Not enough to distract him from the terror of what Willow might be suffering, though.

Majestic cedars, their massive trunks roadblocks, forced him and Star to weave their way through the woods. Theo didn't care. He'd find a way to sprout wings and fly if he had to. He would do anything to find Willow and make things right between them. He knew, deep inside, he had to make it right with God, as well.

"Dear Lord, please, guide me to Willow," Theo murmured beneath his breath. "Please forgive me for my pride, for my wallowing in self-pity and not trusting Willow with my sorrow and grief. For not trusting You with my shame."

His chest heaved with the exertion of climbing over and around the undergrowth. Pausing briefly to get his bearings, he realized they were climbing upward, and the area seemed vaguely familiar. Maybe he and Willow had been through here, yet he didn't remember going off trail like this. Or zigzagging around tight clusters of hemlock or decaying cedars that had long since fallen from age and the weight of moss covering every inch of bark.

Suddenly the trees began to thin, and through the canopy of branches he glimpsed sunlight glinting off the Blue Glacier in the distance. That's why this area seemed familiar. He had been here with Willow years ago. Only the trail they had taken hadn't made the approach from this direction.

The tree line gave way to a wide meadow with tall grass swaying in a slight breeze that stretched to the ridge of an old washout that had happened long before he or Willow had ever been born. The sight that greeted him made his heart stutter with fear.

Near the edge of the ridge, Willow lay on the ground with Charles Zimmer hulking over her. Even from this distance Theo could see Charles had a knife pressed to her throat.

Every instinct in Theo roared for him to charge at Charles, but Theo was too far away. His approach would be too exposed. He would be seen long before he could reach the other man. Charles could easily slice the blade through Willow's skin, severing her arteries and spilling her blood. Just the thought nearly made Theo physically ill.

Star rammed into Theo's leg, forcing his attention to her. She ran to the end of her leash, heading back into the woods.

He didn't understand what the dog wanted. Staying in the deep shadows of the trees, he shook his head at Star and reeled the leash in, forcing Star to retreat. She grabbed the leather strap between her teeth and shook her head as if trying to dislodge the leash from his grasp.

Understanding dawned. She wanted off her leash.

He'd seen this behavior before when Willow and Star had done training with Peyton. Willow had complied, allowing Star off leash to do a search for hidden explosives on her own. Had the dog picked up the scent of explosives?

A fresh wave of fright tore through Theo.

He knelt behind the wide trunk of a tree and grabbed Star's collar. "We have to protect Willow."

Theo turned his attention back to where Charles was dragging Willow to her feet.

A dark spot on the ground snagged Theo's attention. Willow's gun. Had he dropped it? Or had she disarmed him at some point? Clearly he'd subdued her before she could run away. Charles bent to scoop up the weapon.

Pride and respect for his wife infused determination into Theo's veins.

With Star's lead in his hand, Theo and Star ran perpendicular to the meadow through the trees, intent on coming out behind Charles. If Theo could get Charles's attention away from Willow, she could get away. Theo made eye contact with Willow. Surprise flared in her eyes. He could see a mix of joy and fear blooming on her face.

He dropped into a crouch, hoping the tall grass would hide them. He unhooked Star's lead and quickly stuffed it into the pocket of his windbreaker before he tugged the dog close and whispered in her ear, "Protect Willow."

He didn't know if the dog understood, but he hoped so. Star was smarter than most people.

Star licked his face, her rough, hot tongue gliding over his jaw.

Theo rose, drawing Charles's attention away from Willow. Theo sensed rather than saw Star stalking through the grass, closing the distance to his partner.

Charles eyed Theo with hostility, then aimed the gun at Willow. He jammed the KA-BAR knife back into his jacket pocket. But his hand wasn't empty when it reappeared. His fingers curled around a small, cylindrical black device with a red button on top.

Theo's heart dropped. A detonator. Where was the explosive?

"Stop right there, agent man. One more step and I push this button. The whole ravine will go kaboom and us along with it."

Theo held up his hands, palms facing out. "Charles, let Willow go."

"No," Charles yelled. "She has to pay. We all have to pay."

Theo swallowed back the bile rising to burn his throat. Without a doubt, Charles was unhinged and on a suicide mission. Theo had no idea how he'd be able to save Willow. He sent up a prayer for God's intervention.

Amazement and wonder flushed through Willow. Theo had found her. The GPS beacon he'd insisted she keep on her person was the most wonderful gift he'd ever given her. Other than their child.

The rest of the PNK9 Unit couldn't be far behind.

Willow breathed in and slowly released her breath through pursed lips in an effort to calm her heart rate. Now was not the time to panic. She glanced to her right at the steep wall of sediment pitching downward to the bottom of the wash. She was too close to the edge. She inched away, hoping Charles would stay distracted by Theo so she could move to steadier ground. Her shoe scraped over an unnatural lump beneath the loose dirt. One of Charles's explosives? She sent up a prayer that she wouldn't accidentally step on an explosive and set it off. She didn't know what kind of device Charles had rigged.

Her mouth tasted of cotton, dry and cloying. Her limbs shook, weak from lack of water and energy. She prayed her child wasn't suffering. She and the baby had to survive. Theo had to survive. And she wouldn't let another moment pass without telling him what was in her heart.

She had to tell him. Tears welled in her eyes as every emotion imaginable clogged her already-parched throat. She tried to speak, but nothing came out.

Using every particle of willpower she possessed, she forced the words she had to say out in a shout. "Theo, I love you. I've always loved you. I'm so sorry for putting conditions on my love. I was wrong. Wrong to ever say you could only be in my life on my terms."

Movement in the tall grass caught Willow's attention. Her breath caught. Could it be…?

A brown and white dog's head popped up over the grass and disappeared again.

Star. Stalking her prey. Homing in on the explosives.

Theo had brought Star with him.

Willow shouldn't be surprised by her partner's actions. Star was trained for this. She had done this before. On Willow and Theo's first case together.

An idea formed. Star was still so far away. Willow needed to give the dog time to get closer.

It was all the impetus Willow needed to pour out her heart—and hopefully distract Charles by barely pausing for breath. She focused on Theo. "That's not the kind of love that Jesus shows us. He accepts us as we are, and I should've accepted you. I should have walked through the hard parts without expectations. I should have worked through the pain with you instead of protecting myself." Tears of regret slipped down her cheek. "I did exactly what I accused you of doing. I put up my own walls. Hid behind my own wants and desires."

"Oh, gag me," Charles said. "What is this?" The derision and confusion on Charles's face was as clear as the sun glinting off the glacier, but Willow didn't care. She needed Theo to know. If Charles was caught up by the drama, the more the better.

"Ignore him," Theo yelled. His tender gaze trapped her so that all she saw was him. "Don't blame yourself. It was all me. There's nothing for you to ask forgiveness for." His voice broke. "Please, can you ever forgive *me*? I was foolish and stubborn and prideful."

He spread his hands wide as if begging her to run into his embrace. But she didn't dare move.

Theo continued, "I love you. I've always loved you, and I always will." His words were a balm to her rent heart. "I should never have built a wall between us. I should've been open with you, trusted you with my grief and sorrow. Trusted you with my shame. I didn't even trust Jesus." Remorse colored his words, making her chest ache.

"But I know better. God loves me. He loves you." Theo's gaze turned to Charles. "He loves you, too, Charles. No matter what you've done in this life. He still loves you."

"No!" Charles screamed, quivering with agitation. Both of his hands shook. Not good. He held her weapon in his right hand, his finger caressing the trigger. His other hand gripped the detonator, his thumb poised over the button. Willow held her breath and lifted a silent prayer.

"God wants nothing to do with me," Charles said. "You can make your peace with the Almighty. He's done nothing but give me grief."

Willow's heart wept at the bitterness consuming Charles. She didn't think there was a way to reach his hardened heart. But God could do wondrous things beyond human conception.

Hoping for one last-ditch effort to appeal to Charles's humanity, she said, "Charles, look at me. God does love you. And He loves us." She gestured between herself and Theo, then put her hand on her abdomen. "And God loves the child growing inside me. If you do this, you're killing an innocent baby."

Charles's face twisted, his hands going to the sides of his head. "No, no, no. No innocents are supposed to die. That was my father's mantra."

"It's a good mantra," Willow said, seeing the streak of brown and white through the grass again. Star was close now. Close enough to strike.

Willow chanced a step toward Charles. Theo did the same, inching subtly closer.

Charles spun to face Willow, putting his back to Theo. His thumb still rested on the detonator and his finger on the trigger of the gun. She sucked in a breath as Theo rushed forward, only to stop abruptly when Charles spun to face him.

"Oh, no, you don't," Charles yelled. "Stay back!"

Theo's hands went up again, but he stood his ground.

"Charles," Willow said, drawing the man's attention. "A baby. An innocent life. You don't want to disappoint your father, do you?"

Practically spitting with anger, Charles screamed, "It's better for the baby to perish with its parents than for it to grow up alone, untethered to the world."

"Like you were untethered when your father died," Willow said, infusing sympathy into her tone. "I was untethered, too. We were both untethered to this world. That's why we gravitated to the park. The place where it happened. The place we want to protect. But you're not protecting it by doing this."

In the distance, the *thwump, thwump* of helicopter rotors nearly brought Willow to her knees. The sound meant backup was on the way. But if Charles detonated the ridge, the blast could take out the helicopter, too.

"Shut up!" Charles screamed. "Stay quiet so I can think."

Star rose from her hiding place in the tall grass, her body stiff and straight, her tail out behind her, her ears back. Willow's heart stuttered. They needed a distraction.

Willow met Theo's gaze again, hoping he could read her thoughts as she said, "Theo, my love. Do you want to dance?"

He cocked his head, then understanding lit the depths of his dark eyes. A smile filled with determination, and love bloomed on his handsome face. "One last dance to solidify our love."

"One, two," Willow said.

"I said, shut up!" Charles waved the gun at them. "Why are you counting?"

"Charles," she said sharply, drawing his focus just as Theo shouted, "Three!"

Charles pivoted toward Theo. Willow sprang into action, closing the distance between her and Charles. She grabbed Charles's hand holding the gun. At the same instant, Theo lunged at Charles, knocking the detonator out of his grip.

The two-pronged assault startled Charles. His head swiveled between them, not sure how to fend them both off.

Willow forced the gun hand in the air, fighting for control. The weapon went off, the loud report echoing through the wash, but she managed to wrest it from his fingers.

And then Star was there, leaping through the air, her whole body slamming into Charles. Willow and Theo both released their holds on the man. He stumbled backward, his feet struggling to find purchase in the soft dirt covering the explosives.

Fearing Star would go over the edge with Charles, Willow screamed, "Off."

Star immediately pushed away from Charles, letting the momentum she'd initiated take Charles to the very edge of the drop. His arms flailed, and he screamed nearly as loud as the gun's earlier discharge.

Theo lunged forward, grabbing a fistful of Charles's shirt, and pulled him back from the brink of death.

Willow's heart stuttered with pride at her husband.

Theo pushed Charles down to the ground face-first before zip-tying his hands behind his back and his feet together.

Charles cursed, his words absorbed by the dirt.

Willow moved away from the edge and the buried explosives and fell to her knees. Star immediately came to her, licking her face and brushing up against her.

Then Theo was there, kneeling in front of her, cupping her cheeks in his hands. "I thought I'd lost you."

"I can't believe you're here," she said at the same time.

Wind created by the helicopter's rotors whipped around them and drew their gazes skyward. The PNK9 Unit helicopter hovered above them then slowly settled in the meadow.

As if on cue, several dogs and officers burst from the tree line and rushed toward them. Willow's heart thumped against her breastbone in gratitude. She spotted Colt Maxwell and his bloodhound, Samson. Danica Hayes and her German shepherd, Hutch, followed closely by all four candidates and their shepherds.

At the far end of the meadow, Willow saw Asher Gilmore with his English springer spaniel, Ruby Orton and her black Labrador, Pepper, along with Isaac McDane and his partner, a beagle named Freddy. Danica emerged from the tree line with her German shepherd at her side.

The chief, Donovan, and another member of the unit, Tanner Ford, with a boxer named Britta, jumped out of the helicopter. Then, amazingly, Peyton Burns, the unit's lead trainer and Willow's friend, hopped out. Only

Jackson was missing, but Willow knew he was on loan to the US Marshals Service.

"This is so incredible," she breathed out. "They're all here."

Pulling her to her feet, Theo snaked an arm around her waist and leaned close. "You're important to everyone. Me, especially."

Overwhelmed by the show of support, she, Star and Theo hurried to meet the chief and the team. They needed to keep them from where the explosives were buried. She didn't know how stable they were and didn't want anyone to set one off accidentally.

"The whole ridge is rigged to explode. There are explosives buried along the edge," Willow told Donovan. "We need to secure the scene."

Donovan gave her a grim nod. "Asher, contact WSP. Get their technicians here, stat!" Donovan called out, referring to the Washington State Patrol's bomb squad.

"On it," Asher replied.

"There's a detonator around here somewhere," Theo said. "I knocked it from Charles's hand." He gestured to the man lying prone on the ground.

Donovan crouched near Charles's head. "Are the explosives only on the ridge?"

"Lawyer!" Charles shouted. "I'm not talking to you until I get to talk to a lawyer."

Shaking his head with clear disgust and frustration, Donovan stood and gave out instructions to the others. "Spread out and find that detonator. Carefully." He motioned for Owen and Tanner to take Charles into custody. "Get him out of here."

While the team fanned out to search for the detonator, the two men lifted Charles to his feet, undid the tie around his ankles, and led him toward the trees.

Willow could only surmise they all had vehicles parked where Charles had left the silver truck. It would be a long hike for them all. She still marveled that the whole team had come to help. "Donovan," Theo said. "Willow's dehydrated and needs to get to a hospital."

"What?" Willow pulled away from him. "I just need a drink of water. I'll be fine." Ruby shoved a bottle of water in her hand. Willow smiled gratefully at her fellow officer and unscrewed the cap. "Thank you, Ruby."

"Of course," Ruby said. "We've got your back."

Willow's heart swelled with gratitude and fondness for her team. She drank from the bottle, the cool liquid welcome. After recapping the bottle, she turned to the chief and said, "I need to stay here and help work the scene."

"Theo is right," Donovan said gently. "You need care. But we do need Star here."

"I can work her," Peyton volunteered. "Star knows me."

Though Willow appreciated her friend's offer and trusted her with Star, she shook her head. "That's not necessary. I'm fine. I'm not going anywhere until we find that detonator."

Donovan nodded his approval.

She and Star moved to search for the device and any other explosives. Theo stayed at her side.

Forty minutes later, just as the state patrol's bomb squad arrived, Star sat, alerted on something in the tall grass. Willow spotted the detonator. Ready to put this behind her, she called out, "Over here."

She gestured to the bomb technicians, who carefully secured the device, then set out to defuse the explosives buried along the ridge.

Thankfully, no other bombs were located during their sweep of the area. Relief cascaded through Willow, followed quickly by fatigue.

Theo wrapped an arm around her waist, and she gratefully leaned into him.

Donovan gestured to Theo. "Get her on the helicopter. Make sure she gets the medical attention she needs."

Willow wouldn't be coddled. "I don't need to go by helicopter. I can hike out."

Donovan got in her face. The gentleness from before was replaced by a stern glare. "Officer Bates, I will not have you lose your baby due to some maniac. You go to the hospital with your husband, and once you and the baby are both cleared by the doctor, then you can return to work. But I don't want to see you until then."

She wasn't about to argue, with everyone staring at her and the chief arching an eyebrow with the clear expectation that she follow orders, and fatigue pulled at her, so she had no choice but to acquiesce. "Okay. I'll go."

Theo tucked Willow close, guiding her and Star to the helicopter. As soon as Star was settled at her feet, Willow put on a headset and leaned back against the cushioned seat with Theo at her side. The chopper lifted into the air and zipped away from the horrifying scene.

It was finally over. But why didn't she feel settled?

A week later, Willow rambled around her home in Port Angeles, waiting to hear from Theo. A few short texts weren't enough. She wanted more.

After her overnight stay in the hospital, the doctor had declared she and the baby were both fine after their ordeal with Charles Zimmer, who was being held in a federal jail without bail. No one had to worry about him terrorizing the park ever again. She'd given her statement to the FBI and wouldn't have to see Charles until his trial, which would be long after the baby's arrival.

Yet Donovan had still put her on leave for the next few weeks, telling her she needed to rest and decide how she wanted to proceed. What did that even mean?

She knew exactly what she wanted in life. She wanted Theo and her baby and to protect the park. Why couldn't she have all those things?

In part because Theo had left again. Returning to DC. He'd said he had some things to deal with there and he would return when he could. What things? Why was he slipping into his old habit of keeping her in the dark?

She'd tried to be patient. But her patience was running out.

Determination and resolve fueled her as she whirled and marched into her bedroom, grabbing her suitcase from the closet and throwing it onto the bed. She unzipped it and started packing.

This time she wouldn't wait for Theo to come home. She was going to go to him and demand…demand what?

No, not demand. More like plead and beg him to come home and salvage their marriage.

As she packed, her hands shook with adrenaline. She would do whatever it took to win her husband back.

A knock followed by Star's excited barking had Willow hurrying to the front door. She looked through the peephole, and her heart jumped into her throat.

With a gasp of delight, she threw open the door.

Theo. Looking so handsome in dress slacks and a button-down shirt. His dark hair had been slicked back. His clean-shaven jaw called to her, making her hands itch to touch his face.

But it was his crooked smile and the love shining in his eyes that had her giving another squeal of delight and throwing her arms around his neck.

"Whoa. I was hoping for a good reception," he murmured in her ear, his arms holding her close. He smelled like sunshine and promises. "But this is more than I'd hoped for."

She covered his face with kisses. Then she stepped back and leveled him with a censuring glare that she really didn't feel. "I wasn't sure you were coming back."

His mouth twitched. "Can I come in?"

Flushing with pleasure, she stepped back. "This is your home. It will always be your home."

He snagged her around the waist, pulled her tight against him and shut the door with his heel. Star wedged herself between them. They laughed, the moment so tender and sweet Willow's knees wobbled.

Theo bent to scratch Star behind the ears, and Willow was consumed with jealousy. She wanted Theo's undivided attention. For the rest of her life. But she waited patiently until Star was satisfied. And soon, she'd have to wait patiently while their child had Theo's attention. It seemed patience was a virtue she would be well versed in as time went on.

Finally, he straightened, wrapping Willow once again in his embrace. A place she never wanted to leave. He stared into her eyes, and love for this man overwhelmed her. Tears burned the backs of her eyes.

"I'm sorry for not being more forthcoming," he said, contrition ringing in his tone. "I'm a work in progress. I promise I'll do better. It's hard to dig out from beneath the ruins of the wall I'd built around myself."

Her heart ached, recalling how she'd accused him of hiding behind a wall. "I promise to do better, too. Not put so many expectations and conditions on you. On us. Love doesn't work that way. And I do love you."

She placed her hands on his strong shoulders. "But is it too much to ask for you to tell me what's going on?"

He took a breath as if bracing himself. "I've spent the past week talking with the FBI psychologist," he confessed. "This time I was honest with her. Filled her in on Xavier's death and my guilt. It did help to unburden myself. She set me up with a therapist here in Port Angeles."

A flutter of hope had her sputtering. "Here? Not DC?"

"Here. Where I live. I transferred back to the Seattle office. All the paperwork went through last night, and I took the red-eye. To get back to you as soon as I could. I'm not leaving you again. No more undercover assignments for me."

Happiness was like a bright and shiny orb circling around her. "I don't know what to say."

"Say you'll take me back. In fact—" He went down on one knee and slipped his fingers into his shirt pocket. Withdrawing a gold band and a beautiful princess-cut diamond surrounded by sapphires, he said, "Say you'll stay married to me."

Her breath caught. Her chest nearly exploded with so many emotions, she couldn't even name them all. He'd hung on to her wedding set, but he'd added the stunning blue stones to her engagement ring. "Oh, you dear, sweet man."

A hopeful and eager expression passed over his face. "Is that a yes?"

She knelt, too, taking his face in her hands. "Yes. A thousand times, yes."

She kissed him. A kiss born of hope and a love that had never truly died, could never die. A kiss filled with the promise of the future.

Star nudged her way between them. They broke apart, laughing and hugging her, too.

Theo slipped the rings on her finger. "Should we have a new ceremony?"

She snuggled close. "I don't need another ceremony. I just need you. And our growing family."

* * * * *

Dear Reader,

Thank you for taking this journey with Willow and Theo Bates as they worked together to protect the forest while also rekindling their love and salvaging their marriage. I took some creative license with the park and the plotline to make an exciting and suspenseful story for you.

And I absolutely adore the stunning setting for this book. The mysterious and magnificent rain forest and the impressive Blue Glacier are both icons of the national park. And the hot springs resort is a must visit, not to mention the rugged beauty of the coastline. The Olympic National Park is a wonderful place for hiking, camping and grand adventures. Hopefully safe ones!

I hope you'll continue with the women and men of the Pacific Northwest K9 Unit as they search for Mara Gilmore and the stolen puppies. You won't want to miss these exciting stories.

To learn more about me and my books, visit my webpage at https://www.terrireed.com/. I'd love for you to sign up for my newsletter. I promise not to bombard you!

Blessings,
Terri Reed

Get 3 FREE REWARDS!

We'll send you 2 FREE Books plus a FREE Mystery Gift.

FREE
Value Over
$20

Both the **Love Inspired**® and **Love Inspired**® **Suspense** series feature compelling novels filled with inspirational romance, faith, forgiveness and hope.

YES! Please send me 2 FREE novels from the Love Inspired or Love Inspired Suspense series and my FREE gift (gift is worth about $10 retail). After receiving them, if I don't wish to receive any more books, I can return the shipping statement marked "cancel." If I don't cancel, I will receive 6 brand-new Love Inspired Larger-Print books or Love Inspired Suspense Larger-Print books every month and be billed just $6.49 each in the U.S. or $6.74 each in Canada. That is a savings of at least 16% off the cover price. It's quite a bargain! Shipping and handling is just 50¢ per book in the U.S. and $1.25 per book in Canada.* I understand that accepting the 2 free books and gift places me under no obligation to buy anything. I can always return a shipment and cancel at any time by calling the number below. The free books and gift are mine to keep no matter what I decide.

Choose one: ☐ **Love Inspired Larger-Print** (122/322 BPA GRPA) ☐ **Love Inspired Suspense Larger-Print** (107/307 BPA GRPA) ☐ **Or Try Both!** (122/322 & 107/307 BPA GRRP)

Name (please print)

Address   Apt. #

City   State/Province   Zip/Postal Code

Email: Please check this box ☐ if you would like to receive newsletters and promotional emails from Harlequin Enterprises ULC and its affiliates. You can unsubscribe anytime.

Mail to the Harlequin Reader Service:
IN U.S.A.: P.O. Box 1341, Buffalo, NY 14240-8531
IN CANADA: P.O. Box 603, Fort Erie, Ontario L2A 5X3

Want to try 2 free books from another series? Call 1-800-873-8635 or visit www.ReaderService.com.

LIRLIS23

Get 3 FREE REWARDS!

We'll send you 2 FREE Books plus a FREE Mystery Gift.

FREE
Value Over
$20

Both the **Harlequin® Special Edition** and **Harlequin® Heartwarming™** series feature compelling novels filled with stories of love and strength where the bonds of friendship, family and community unite.

YES! Please send me 2 FREE novels from the Harlequin Special Edition or Harlequin Heartwarming series and my FREE Gift (gift is worth about $10 retail). After receiving them, if I don't wish to receive any more books, I can return the shipping statement marked "cancel." If I don't cancel, I will receive 6 brand-new Harlequin Special Edition books every month and be billed just $5.49 each in the U.S. or $6.24 each in Canada, a savings of at least 12% off the cover price, or 4 brand-new Harlequin Heartwarming Larger-Print books every month and be billed just $6.24 each in the U.S. or $6.74 each in Canada, a savings of at least 19% off the cover price. It's quite a bargain! Shipping and handling is just 50¢ per book in the U.S. and $1.25 per book in Canada.* I understand that accepting the 2 free books and gift places me under no obligation to buy anything. I can always return a shipment and cancel at any time by calling the number below. The free books and gift are mine to keep no matter what I decide.

Choose one: ☐ **Harlequin Special Edition**
(235/335 BPA GRMK)

☐ **Harlequin Heartwarming Larger-Print**
(161/361 BPA GRMK)

☐ **Or Try Both!**
(235/335 & 161/361 BPA GRPZ)

Name (please print)

Address   Apt. #

City   State/Province   Zip/Postal Code

Email: Please check this box ☐ if you would like to receive newsletters and promotional emails from Harlequin Enterprises ULC and its affiliates. You can unsubscribe anytime.

Mail to the Harlequin Reader Service:
IN U.S.A.: P.O. Box 1341, Buffalo, NY 14240-8531
IN CANADA: P.O. Box 603, Fort Erie, Ontario L2A 5X3

Want to try 2 free books from another series? Call 1-800-873-8635 or visit www.ReaderService.com.

*Terms and prices subject to change without notice. Prices do not include sales taxes, which will be charged (if applicable) based on your state or country of residence. Canadian residents will be charged applicable taxes. Offer not valid in Quebec. This offer is limited to one order per household. Books received may not be as shown. Not valid for current subscribers to the Harlequin Special Edition or Harlequin Heartwarming series. All orders subject to approval. Credit or debit balances in a customer's account(s) may be offset by any other outstanding balance owed by or to the customer. Please allow 4 to 6 weeks for delivery. Offer available while quantities last.

Your Privacy—Your information is being collected by Harlequin Enterprises ULC, operating as Harlequin Reader Service. For a complete summary of the information we collect, how we use this information and to whom it is disclosed, please visit our privacy notice located at corporate.harlequin.com/privacy-notice. From time to time we may also exchange your personal information with reputable third parties. If you wish to opt out of this sharing of your personal information, please visit readerservice.com/consumerschoice or call 1-800-873-8635. Notice to California Residents—Under California law, you have specific rights to control and access your data. For more information on these rights and how to exercise them, visit corporate.harlequin.com/california-privacy.

HSEHW23

HARLEQUIN
PLUS

Try the best multimedia subscription service for romance readers like you!

Read, Watch and Play.

Experience the easiest way to get the romance content you crave.

Start your **FREE TRIAL** at
<u>www.harlequinplus.com/freetrial</u>.